THE BOOK OF THE BEAST

TANITH LEE

THE BOOK OF THE BEAST

THE SECRET BOOKS OF PARADYS II

THE OVERLOOK PRESS
WOODSTOCK, NEW YORK

First paperback published in 1997 by
The Overlook Press
Lewis Hollow Road
Woodstock, New York 12498

Library of Congress Cataloging-in-Publication Data

Lee, Tanith
The book of the beast: the secret books of Paradys II / Tanith Lee
p. cm.
I. Title.
PR6062.E4163B65
823'.914—dc20   90-48488   CIP
Manufactured in the United States of America
Originally published in the United Kingdom by Unwin Hyman Ltd.
ISBN: 0-87951-698-4
987654321

Contents

THE GREEN BOOK

eyes like emerald

PART ONE

The Scholar

She with apples you desired
From Paradise came long ago:
With you I feel that if required,
Such still within my garden grow.
                              Shelley

By the end of the first night, he knew that his lodging was
haunted. From the night's first minute, he should have
guessed.

A hag greeted him on the threshold.

'M'sire Raoulin?' squawked she in her old-fashioned
way. And in the dusk she held high one quavering candle.
He learned at once by that the interior would be ill-lit.

'I am Raoulin. My baggage and chest have arrived?'

'You are to follow me,' she said, like a portress of the
damned in Hell, who could not be expected to have luggage.

'To my host, your master?'

She said, 'There's no master here. There's no one here.
M'sire No One is the lord in these parts.'

She led him in across a black cavern of a hall, over a
blacker courtyard, up an outer stair, in at an arch, along two
or three corridors, and in the light-watered darkness opened
for him a wooden door with her keys. When she had lit a
pair of candles in his apartment, she told him she would
bring his supper in an hour, or if he liked company he might
partake below in the kitchen with herself and the groom.
Plainly he was not royalty, and she intended him to see she
knew it.

3

Out of malicious curiosity therefore he said he would dine below. She gave him directions he was sure he would forget.

'And mind out, on the stair,' she said.

'Mind what?'

'For M'sire No One,' she replied, and cackled.

She was a cheery eerie old soul.

Raoulin was a tall, well-made young man, good-looking in his ivory-ebony mode, for he was by stock a black-haired northerner. His father owned horses and cattle, vineyards, orchards and numberless fields, and in the long low house, while the other sons toiled at the land or galloped off wenching, there was Raoulin, constricted by tutors. They swelled his brain with Latin and fair Greek, they made inroads on his spirit with philosophy and hints alchemical. Raoulin was to go to the City and study at the university of the Sachrist.

When the hour came, he was not sorry. He had been set apart from his family by increasing erudition. It had come to pass he could not sneeze without being accused of some sophistry or conundrum. For the City, he had heard it was packed with churches, libraries and brothels. It was the epitome of all desired wickedness: teases for the intellect, pots for the flesh.

The lodging was arranged via his father's steward, who told him only the place had been, a decade before, a great palace, the home of the noble house of d'Uscaret. They had fallen on hard times, through some political out-management, the steward believed. For the mighty families of the City had, even ten years before, been constantly engaged with one another, fighting their blood-feuds on the streets and cutting each other's throats besides in the Duke's council chamber.

Certain members of tribe d'Uscaret were still supposed to live in the mansion. It was said to be dilapidated but also sumptuous. A prestigious residence, a good address.

But no sooner had Raoulin ridden along the narrow twilight street and seen the towers of the manse arising behind their ruinously walled gardens; the ornate, unillumined facade, like that of some antique tomb, than he was sure of poverty, plagues of mice and lice, and that the steward of his father, altogether fonder of the other sons, had done him a bad turn.

Supper was not so bad, a large vegetable dish with rice, and a gooseberry gelatine, pancakes, and ale. Though money had been provided for his fare, Raoulin was not sure he would not be cheated. As it was, grandma tucked in heartily, and the bony groom, smacking lips and clacking their three or four teeth like castanets.

'Perhaps,' said Raoulin, 'you might get me some beef tomorrow.'

'Maybe, if beef's to be had. And my poor legs aren't fit for running up and down to the meat market,' replied grandma.

'Then send the girl,' said Raoulin casually. 'And by the by, I hope you'll see she's fed too.'

A silence greeted this.

Raoulin poured himself more ale.

The groom sat watching him like a motheaten old wolf, dangerous for all his dearth of fangs. The hag peered fiercely from her mashed plate.

'We have no girl. He and I, is all.'

'Then, she's the lady of the house. I beg her pardon.'

In fact, he had not thought her a servant, not for one minute. It had been a test.

Now the hag said again, 'Only us. And yourself.'

'And M'sire No One. Yes, I recall. But in the corridors I passed this lady. A maiden, I believe.'

Then the groom spoke. He said, 'That can't be, for let me tell you, sieur, there's no other living soul in this house saving we and you.'

'Oh, a ghost, then,' said Raoulin.

His heart jumped, not unpleasantly. He did not believe in

ghosts, therefore longed to have their being proved to him, like the existence of God.

He had of course lost himself on emerging from his apartment. There were no lights anywhere, only the worm-runs of windowless corridors on which the occasional door obtruded. Now and then, from perversity, he had tried these doors. Three gave access to barren chambers, empty of nearly anything. One had a shuttered window, another a candle-branch standing on the floor. (The branch was of iron, worth little. The candle-stubs had long ago been devoured by vermin.) A few other doors resisted his impulse. He fancied they were stuck rather than locked. Presently he reached an ascending stair he was certain he had not seen on entry with the hag. He paused in irritated perplexity, wondering if it would be worthwhile to climb. Just then a woman appeared and went across the stair-top, evidently negotiating the corridor which ran parallel to that below.

She did not carry a candle, and that he saw her at all was due to his own light, and the pallor of her hair and skin which caught it. Her gown was of some sombre stuff, high-waisted as was now not always the fashion, and she held her hands joined under her breast. A stiff silver net contained her hair; it glittered sharply once as she glided by. That was all. She was gone literally in that flash. Her face he did not really see, yet her slightness, something about her, made him think her girlish.

Anyone else, going over the unlit upper corridor, must have glanced downward at his light. Not she.

He had lacked the impertinence to pursue.

He waited all through supper to see if any reference would be made to the fair passager – he had decided she was attractive; she had to be, being mysterious.

'And if she is a ghost,' he continued, 'whose ghost?'

The groom and the old woman exchanged looks. Raoulin had seen such before. The camaraderie of age against youth, stupid cunning against stupid intelligence, the low against the better who was not better enough to get respect.

'There's no ghost here,' said the old woman at length. 'You were dreaming, your head full of scholar books.'

'All right,' said Raoulin, pleased by the heightening Stygian shade of deception, faithfully observed as in any romance. 'Probably a trick of the candle.'

Returning towards his rooms, he tried for the fork of the corridor where he had lost himself and found the stair.

He could not regain it.

Having gone up and down and round and about for quite an hour, having peered into further fruitless rooms of dust, mouse-cities, broken furniture, he only rediscovered his rightful corridor with difficulty. His heart, which had begun by beating excitedly, was now leaden with weariness. Reaching his bed, thank God aired with hot stones, he flung himself among the sheets and barely had space to blow out the candle before he was asleep.

Here, unconscious, he dreamed the door to his apartment was stealthily opened. A slim shadow drifted over the outer chamber. He sensed it examining as it went the closed travelling chest, the books he had already set out, a small reliquary his mother had pressed upon him. Then, entering the bedroom, all in black night, the shadow cast around. White fingers, that glimmered in the void, traced his doublet where he had thrown it down, a purse of coins – he heard them chink – his dagger – he longed to warn her to be careful, the edge was newly honed.

Then to the brink of his bed she stole, this immoderate phantom.

In utter black, through sleep and closed eyelids, yet he made her out.

A mask of Parsuan porcelain floated above him in a silver-grilled aureole-light of blondest hair. As he had known it must be, the face was lovely, and cool as snow. And the eyes – ! Never had Raoulin seen such eyes. Wide-set, carved a touch slantingly, fringed with pale lashes, and very clear.

7

And oh, their colour. They were like the jewels he remembered from a bishop's mitre, two matching emeralds, green as two linden leaves against the sun.

Asleep, miles off, Raoulin attempted to order his body to speak to her. But the words could not be dredged up from the sea, his lips and tongue refused obedience.

Drowning, he could only gaze on her as she drew aside from him, swimming far away, over the horizon of night.

One day remained to Raoulin before he must present himself at the university. How he regretted its brevity. He had meant to use the time in exploration of the wicked City of Paradys, but now a morning sufficed for this. He visited the markets, and pried amongst the crannied shops, saw the shining coils of the river straddled by bridges, gazed on the great grey Temple-Church of the Sacrifice, where he must hear at least one Mass and report the fact to his mother.

By early afternoon he had strayed back south-west of the City, to gloomy House d'Uscaret.

In daylight, the upland streets – the mansion was on one of the many hills that composed Paradys – were not appetising. Nothing fell so low as the highmost. There were other large houses and imposing towers in the area, now gone to tenements, tiles off, stones crumbling, strung with torn washing. In the alleys was disgusting refuse. Every crevice seemed to hold debris or the bones of small deceased animals.

Having gained the house by a side entry, to which the hag had given him a key, Raoulin set himself to master the building.

He had determined to recover the ghost's corridor, and all through the hot post-noon he sought it, and, wide-awake, finally found it, too. The corridor seemed redolent yet of her ghostly fragrance. And shivering slightly, he started along in the direction she had chosen. Soon enough it gave on a further flight of ascending steps – perhaps the spectre had a

8

lair . . . But the solitary door above was disappointingly jammed – or secured – Raoulin could only concede that this kept up the best traditions of romance.

Then came another fall of stairs leading down, with, at their head, a slit of window covered by a grille. Looking out, Raoulin realised himself to be in a tall tower of the house. He saw the pebbled slope of roofs, and, to his surprise, noticed the distant miniature of the Temple-Church adrift like a promontory in soft haze.

Taking the downward stair, he next arrived against a low door, which for an amazement opened.

There lay a garden, walled apart from the rest.

It had been made for a woman, he supposed; even through the riot of weeds and ivy, a map of vestal symmetry was apparent. A garden of more southern climes, modelled, maybe, on the classical courts of the Roman. Clipped ilex and conifer that had burst from shape, a tank of marble all green with lichen and with a green velvet scum upon it. The wrecks of arbours were visible, and a charming statue, a young girl in a graceful tunic, holding up an archaic oil-lamp which once it had been possible to kindle.

Raoulin trod down paths, breaking the skeins of creeper with his elegant shoes, the ivy trying to detain him by clutching at the points of his sleeves and hose.

No birds sang in that garden of emerald green. He knew it had been made for her – or that she had made it her own.

Therefore, he was not startled, reaching the end of an avenue, to confront the bank of yew in which gaped a black frontage: the arched portico of a mausoleum.

The tomb was not very big, nor very old, quite fresh. He read with ease the name on the arch in its bannering of stone. While, student-scholar that he was, he had no trouble either with the Latin underneath.

Helise d'Uscaret
Brought a bride to this House
Now at the court of Death below

A huge lock maintained the entrance of the tomb. But, thought Raoulin, leaning on a tree, a ghost could pass straight through all walls, of wood, iron or granite.

Useless then to fasten up his own chamber. Even had he dreamed of doing so.

He wished to be served his supper that night in his rooms. He did not question the hag. He told her nothing. He did not even note she had put some morsels of beef into his stew, as requested.

During the evening, he glanced upon a few books, and partly turned his mind towards the morning. But the Sachrist had lost its stature.

In a strange condition he took himself early to bed, soon after the City bells had rung the Hesperus. (He would need to rise at Prima Hora.)

He lay on his back, besieged by sensuality, and lovely listless desires that had no need to exert themselves or to hold back. Lethargy stole slowly but certainly upon him, the harbinger. Sleep came in drifts, easily, totally, before the window had quite darkened.

But she, *she* did not come at all.

Though he had been trained to be something of a thinker, Raoulin was not properly a dreamer. Where he inclined to poetry, it was the cadence of the moment.

The ghost had failed to keep their assignation, and continued to fail.

Within a month, unsupplied by anything further uncanny, and by then thoroughly embroiled in the student life of the university, Raoulin had put the green-eyed haunt aside. It is true that he referred privately to the house as "bewitched", and even once in conversation with a fellow student had described his address as "d'Uscaret the ghost mansion." But the fellow student had only absently remarked that among the desuetudinous old houses of Ducal times,

there were scarcely any that did not have either a phantom
or a curse.

By day the university, which was run rather on the classical lines, worked its claws into his brain, and Raoulin
caught a fever of learning only before intimated. By night he
had now friends of the same feather, unlike his leery
brothers, with whom to go debating and drinking. More
often than not, as the first month enlarged to a plural,
Raoulin did not bother to sup at his lodging, but dined in
some cheap tavern with his comrades, went to a cock-fight,
or to watch in their season the street players, who would set
up their stages under the walls of the Sacrifice, or such com-
memorative plague churches as Our Lady of Ashes. His
head was either burnished with wine or bright with ideas,
the licence or strictures of Petronius, Petrarch, and Pliny the
Other, the miracles of Galen. Raoulin was aware he was
happy, but wisely, like a superstitious savage in some
travelogue of the Caesars, did not name his state.

With the wine-shops and bookshops and passing shows,
temporal or religious, he was soon familiar. Not so after all
with the brothels. Some caution from home had stuck, concerning dread diseases, and heartless females intent only on
robbery. Raoulin had been accustomed to the wholesome
but difficult girls of the village, or to celibacy perforce.

The ghost had fired his blood, but that was only to be
expected. Women were the Devil's, and if dead or damned,
their power must be irresistible. You could not be blamed
for fancying a ghost.

But the phantom came no more to tickle him in helpless
sleep.

Instead it was Joseph who caught his arm and said,
'Tomorrow is a Holy Day.'

'Good. Let us be holy,' replied Raoulin.

Joseph laughed, and the dark sunlight of evening glinted
on his eye-glasses and the silver tags of his points – for
Joseph was not poor.

'I had another notion in mind. Over the river is a tavern, by name the *Black Smith*. Behind lies a house which calls itself the *Sweet Cup*.'

'Ah ha,' said Raoulin cautiously.

'The girls are clean, you have my word,' said Joseph. 'I've been there.'

'I have a treatise on the fifth humour – '

'First come and console the possibly non-existent other four. The world is for man's enjoyment.'

On the board of the tavern was a mighty Nubian – the eponymous smith – who, swinging high his hammer, was about to crush the noddle of a fallen enemy sprawled across the anvil. Raoulin regarded this sign with interest, disfavour, and amusement. They drank no more than a token goblet, however, before going through a hind door and out across a yard. Here a ladder had been fixed, seeming to ascend into a hayloft. 'What kind of pastoral cubby is this?' demanded Raoulin jollily: the one goblet had been of the strong kind. 'Never fear, you shall see wonders,' answered Joseph.

They managed the ladder and so got into the loft. It seemed bare, and they crossed in near blackness.

The far end of the loft gave them a shut door. Joseph knocked loudly in five spaced raps.

Presently a tiny aperture, like the spy-hole of a nunnery, was opened, and someone looked out at them invisibly. A woman's voice inquired: 'Who is there?'

'Two men.'

'Are you thirsty?' asked the voice.

'For a sweet cup,' said Joseph.

Apparently all this was in the nature of a password. The door of the brothel came unbarred, and they were let through.

Raoulin stared. He was in a lobby, the plaster of whose walls was covered by paintings of a vivid and obscene nature.

12

There a shepherd disrobed a shepherdess by means of his crook, there a minstrel, his curvaceous viol put by, gently bowed the naked breasts of a lady instead – and there a priapic faun frolicked with two dryads in garlands of grapes and vine leaves. Swerving about from this, Raoulin encountered the door-keeper herself, who was startlingly clad in the draped garment of an antique Roman lady, a thing of such fine gauze that through it every contour, glint and shade of her otherwise nudity might be seen.

This nymph greeted them with an Eastern flourish.

'Will you drink of the bowl of joy?'

'We *will*,' said Joseph.

The nymph ran her glance across Raoulin. Her eyes were edged with kohl and her cheeks powdered. Her face had on more clothing than her body.

'Do you know the custom of the house?'

Joseph nodded. Raoulin, his blood thundering in his ears, was prepared to learn it.

From a pedestal the nymph raised a large cup of white ceramic. She held it out before them.

Joseph reached in a hand, and plucked something forth.

'Take a counter,' he said to Raoulin. 'That's how you select your girl.'

'What? Unseen? Suppose she's not to my taste – '

The nymph said to him smoothly, flirtatiously, 'Every one of our damsels is beautiful.'

'Whose word do I have?' (Joseph wriggled uneasily.) 'What if,' said Raoulin, primed still by the one strong goblet, 'I prefer you?'

But just then he became aware of a man stirring in the shadow of a curtain beyond the paintings. Big and black he looked, like the smith off the tavern sign. So Raoulin shrugged, paid as Joseph did what he was asked, and took a small square counter like a die from the cup.

The nymph, while she had not responded to his sally, did

13

not seem to dislike him for it. She said to Joseph, 'You know the way, sieur. I'll guide your friend.'

Then the curtain was drawn aside (the bully had effaced himself) and they entered a corridor. It appeared to run back a long way, and its sides were made mostly of high wooden screens which creaked mysteriously and emitted driblets of light. Although the screens were occlusive, weird shadows had been flung up on the low uneven ceiling, tangles of writhing knots, like serpents. And there were sounds too, perhaps like the noises in Hell, gasps and grunts, squeals and moans, and now and then a cry, a blasphemy, a prayer.

Raoulin was filled by apprehension as by lust. They had long since become, these two emotions, mutually conducive.

Suddenly Joseph slunk aside. He went through one of the screens and was consumed into the abyss.

The door-keeper had not looked at the counter Raoulin selected, perhaps it made no difference. She led him unerringly, and all at once the corridor was crossed by a pair of aisles. These were both of them in darkness. The nymph halted, and pointed to the left-hand way.

'Yes?' said Raoulin uncertainly.

'Yes, m'sieur,' said the door-keeper. And reaching up, she kissed him on the lips with a little snake's flicker of the tongue. 'The very last of the doors. It's marked with the same mark as on the counter. For you, something special.'

Then she was gone, leaving him alight with the thirst of the house.

He went into the corridor and saw that it did indeed have doors rather than screens. The last of these, blundered on in the gloom, was marked with – what was it? A sort of mask . . . He did not wait for more, but pushed at the barrier. It swung open with a lubricious croak.

Again, Raoulin had pause.

There was a pale-washed room with an Eastern carpet on one wall, the floor very clean, and lightly strewn with colourless flower-heads picked for their scent, as in a lady's chamber. One felt one had stumbled into the wrong house. Against another wall stood a couch, perhaps too wide for virginity; yet otherwise this was all the stuff of a well-to-do and pure girl's bedroom – even to the straightbacked chair and the little footstool. These, turned a fraction away from the door, were occupied.

Raoulin's heart, ready engorged like his loins, took a leap. Was it all some jest – some mischief – but how would Joseph have known – ?

Raoulin closed the door with stealth, and began to walk silently forward, his heart noisy, and prepared for anything –

As he circled like a fox, the posed picture came visible, the chair and the girl seated in it, her blonde head slightly bent, her face dippered into shadow . . .

She wore a black gown, but its lacing, at the bosom not the back, had been loosed, and under it there was no modest "breast-plate" of embroidered linen or silk, only the silken pressure of two breasts. Her feet were bare upon the stool, and nearly all one leg, the skirt of the gown caught up as if through negligence. Her left hand lay idly at her throat, just above the portion of white flesh that rose, swelled and tugged at the laces of the bosom, and sank down, leaving them slackened. The right hand rested upon an object which nestled at her belly. It was a skull.

Here was a maiden discovered alone and untrammelled, her hem carelessly raised, but in the most solemn act of contemplation advocated by the church: dwelling upon the martyrdom of the saints, and on the personal death. *To this shall you come.*

But her face – whose face was it?

At that instant, as if quietly wakening from a dream, she lifted her head.

Despite the blondness, and the skull, she was not Helise d'Uscaret.

Raoulin shuddered. He was dreadfully relieved and sorry.

It was a pretty face, too innocent, with a weak kissable mouth, and cool weasel eyes that knew everything.

She had seen him shudder, and she said in a whisper, 'Thinking of death makes me remember life.'

And she took his hands and put one upon the skull and the other upon her left breast.

So warm one, and beating itself with a heart, and the other as cold and hard as a stone.

'We're only mortal,' said the girl. 'How constricting are these laces – '

For a moment he could not unclamp his hands, from the icy apple of corruption, the hot fluttering apple of quickness.

But she released him and drew his fingers to her laces.

Then, the skull had rolled down into the flowers and he knelt between the bared limb and the covered one, his hands sliding on the treasures of Eve, and her hands, not those of a maiden, everywhere upon him, so he could hardly bear it.

She showed him how he might have her in the chair, if he wished, and he could not wait another second.

As he united with her, the whole room seemed to thunder. He had not had a girl for half a year.

She urged him on with wild cries that, in his tumult, he believed. As the spasm shook him, he kicked the damnable skull, and it rattled away across the floor.

'Have I pleased you?'

'Oh, yes.'

'Then . . . will you give me a little gift – ?'

Raoulin frowned. He had paid at the door and reckoned this unsuitable. But then again, perhaps they robbed their girls here, and it had been very good. If he tipped her, she might let him have her again, although she had already gone behind a curtain to wash, and she came back with her laces tied, and he supposed his time with her was up.

He put a coin between her breasts, and leaned to kiss

her. She allowed it. But then she said, 'I regret. The Mother's strict.'

'*Mother* – what, of your nunnery?'

The blonde whore lowered her eyes. But she removed his hands.

'Unkindness,' he said. 'No charity.'

'It isn't my choice. In a minute I shall be wanted.'

'And if I protest, that hulk of a door-fellow will throw me out.'

She said nothing.

Raoulin straightened his clothes and did up his points with surly tardiness. 'This is a churlish place. I won't come back. Even the old hag's more friendly at d'Uscaret.'

No sooner had he uttered this than he was puzzled at having done so. To name his lodging to a chance harlot would not, even in the nicest circumstances, have seemed sensible to him. But there, too late, it was said.

He expected no response. Perhaps she would have the grace to be deaf.

But then she asked, in a peculiar tone, 'How is it called?'

'What?'

'Your lodging is it? *There*?'

'Where?' And now he looked up with a merry smile – and met the eyes of a terrified animal in a trap. 'Why – what's up with you?'

'D'Uscaret?' she said. 'Is it *there*?'

'Possibly I may have – '

'You lodge *there*?'

She was so insistent she seemed to drive him.

'Very well, I do. But don't try to make anything of it – '

Before he had even finished, she began to scream.

He stood astounded, without a thought in his head. It seemed to be occurring in another room, this appalling outcry and madness – for while she screamed she ran about, threw herself at the walls, tore at herself with her nails in the most horrible way – dragged down the costly carpet from the plaster and writhed with it on the ground.

As had to happen next, the door burst open. Two roughs, one with drawn dagger, came shouldering through. The larger, unarmed, man seized Raoulin, while his companion laid the dagger under Raoulin's ear.

Raoulin kept quite still. He said firmly, 'I did nothing to her that wasn't natural. We were talking after – and then this!' He had to raise his voice, for she went on shrieking, though now her vocal chords cracked. The doorway filled with clusters of frightened or curious male and female faces. A girl, clad only in a shift, pushed by and ran to the blonde harlot, tried to take hold of her and quieten her. It was beyond her powers. Two others hastened to join the struggle, calling the blonde pet names as they ripped her ripping hands from her hair and breasts –

Then the proprietress, the ''Mother'', was in the room, a pockmarked frump one would not turn to regard once on the street.

'Explain this hubbub.'

Her presence bore such authority, even the demented creature on the floor grew abruptly mute, and then began to weep. The three other girls cradled her.

The Mother turned her unadorable gaze on Raoulin.

'Well?'

Raoulin thought quickly. Only the bizarre truth would do. He reluctantly rendered it. ' – And when I told her d'Uscaret – '

'*D'Uscaret*!' exclaimed the woman. Her face had altered. She did not look afraid, but a wily sort of blankness was stealing over her, the appearance she would put on for the confessional.

Raoulin took heart. He said boldly, 'This isn't what I called *here* for.'

'No, no doubt not. There's some superstition, concerning that house. An old curse. I'm surprised my girl knows of it.'

Abruptly the blonde harlot raised her raw voice in another spewing of screams.

'Be silent!' cried the Mother. And the screams went to weeping again.

'Let him be,' she added to her roughs. And to Raoulin himself, with all the casualness of cunning unease, 'And you, sieur, had best get off.'

As the slabby hands released him, Raoulin caught in the doorway now the wink of Joseph's humiliated and resentful spectacles.

Crossing the bridge in the torchlight, between one dark bank and the other, Joseph lamented, 'I can never go back there now.'

'Do you want to? We find it's a hospital for lunatics not a bawdy,' said Raoulin, obscurely embarrassed.

'Frightening a silly trollop with your foul story – '

'I *told* no story. I said that name – d'Uscaret – and all the hordes of Hell broke loose. I can tell you, any fun I had wasn't worth *that*.'

They parted unaffectionately on the upper bank. Laude was ringing softly from Our Lady of Ashes. The river flexed its gleaming muscles. Raoulin was sorry to have lost Joseph's regard. Probably tomorrow, or in a few days, they would laugh about the affair.

Yet somewhere inside his head as he climbed the hills, the awful screams of the harlot rang on and on. One believed she might have seen and heard and done a thing or two. Whatever had made her afraid was something proportionally horrible.

Going under the Sacrifice, beneath the winged cliffs of its buttresses, he considered his lodging. He considered the ghost he might only have dreamed. Was it that?

Some late revellers from a tavern roiled by with lanterns. They seemed to have come from another world than the darkness in which he moved, through which he climbed, and to which he went.

And then, as he entered the twisting alley that led up

to the back walls of the house, he saw the black tower-tops, and the one black turreted tower with a faint greenish firefly-light flickering in it.

Raoulin stopped as if he had met the Medusa's petrifying head. For a moment he could not breathe.

The tower was that which looked north, towards the Temple-Church – the tower into which he had penetrated the first day, trying its one door that would not open. The tower whose stair gave on the weedy garden and the tomb.

How ominous the light looked there, dim and shifting behind its pane of corrupt glass. Did someone move in the room, up and down?

Had he the spirit now to go in and seek the chamber, to push wide the door and maybe find there a young woman in a chair, her hand upon a skull . . .

Raoulin broke into a chill sweat. To his dismay he realised he too was frightened. He remembered the porcelain face of his dream and the cat's-eyes of perfect emerald hovering above him – and marked himself with the sign of the cross. 'The Lord is my keeper. The sun shall not smite me by day, nor the moon by night – ' And, at the side door, unlocking it, whispered: 'Be not afraid for the terror by night, nor for the arrow that flieth . . .'

To the kitchen he went, and lit there two of the candles and stuck them on the spikes of a branch. This he carried before him. Somewhere the hag and the groom snored in aged sleep. They were not juicy enough for demons to chew –

He crowded such ideas from him, and crept like a scared child up through thick night to his apartment. And there he locked the door, and there, by the shine of many extravagant wicks, he opened the reliquary his pious mother had sent with him, and took out the bones and the nails of the saint, and kissed them.

And in bed he recalled that to go with a whore was a sin and if he died tonight, the Devil would get him.

So at length he slept and had nightmares, but nothing else of the quick or the dead approached.

In the morning came summer sunlight, and the now familiar sounds and stenches of the summer city. Birds chimed past the window. Raoulin lay in the warm brightness of the reborn earth and called himself a dunce.

Too timid to go to the tower by night. Well, he would go there presently and smash in the door if he must.

It was even a Holy Day, God watchful.

In the kitchen, where he broke his fast, the hag pottered about. An evil grey cat, thin as a string and kept for the mice, hissed at him from the hearth like an adder.

'Well, puss,' said Raoulin to the cat, 'I'm off to watch the priests and processions. Is it a fact, granny,' he added for the hag's full benefit, 'they carry a Christ out of the Sacrifice made all of alabaster and silver, with wounds of malachite?'

'Go see,' said the hag.

He promised he would, but instead of course made straight for the yard stair and the rooms of the hinder house.

Again, he had difficulty locating the exact spot. Then on the proper steps, up in the correct passage, confronting the solitary door, in the dark, doubt wormed under his skin, his flesh *crawled*. Until, turning, he saw – as if he had reinvented it – the slit of window above the garden stair, and day and daytime Paradys (in which reverential bells were ringing, to encourage him). He went and drank in the vista, like a draught of medicine. Then returned up into the passageway. Here he tried the door again, courteously. As before, it was immovable. It was a formidable bastion, too, looked at with an eye to damage. The timbers were heavy, and thewed with iron.

Dunce again. He had brought no implement to help him.

But then there was the adjacent garden, some handy bough or up-levered stone would do the job.

He was on the garden stair, descending, past the window and into shadow, when he heard a noise above.

Raoulin clamped himself against the wall. His lips formed a prayer. He thrust it off angrily. This was broad day. No non-existent fiend had power now –

What he had heard was the sigh of a woman's skirt, sweeping along the corridor. Then his heart roared loudly enough he could scarcely hear anything else – until the rasp of a turning key somehow reached him.

The big obdurate door was being breached, and Raoulin could no longer cower there in ignorance. He went back up the stair, crouching like a toad, and peered above the top step.

The doorway gaped. It was a gap of paleness, not dark, a chamber lit by a window. That was, from this quirky vantage, all he could see.

And then, out of the door walked the hag.

Over one arm she bore some bed-linen, and in her other hand a platter on which there balanced a costly goblet of glass. There were some dregs of murky fluid in it, some brackish wine.

Not looking about, the hag proceeded along the corridor, and as she did this the door swung suddenly shut, and again he heard the note of a key turning in a lock.

Raoulin sat himself on the stair. He was grinning, bemused, disturbed, but no longer afraid. Did a ghost require wine and food and fresh linen? Did a ghost lock itself in by hand?

A voluntary prisoner lurked within the tower. The lady of d'Uscaret was a recluse. They had said no one lived here, to confound the lodger. But, by the Mass, it was his own father's coin went to feed her now. He had some say in her doings.

He half resolved at once to burst upon her. The hag must have a secret knock. He would have to batter in the door, explain the act as a notion of rescue in ignorance. After all, she could not have reported or complained of his previous attempts.

In a moment he thought better of this idiocy. There were other ways to come at her. Whoever she was, she was not Helise, the dead bride. He had only glimpsed her, for that dream, he saw now, was only a dream. Perhaps the reality was old, toothless and ugly. Be careful. He would spy, and woo her slowly, to see if she was worth the effort.

With an abrupt easing of the heart, Raoulin ran up the stair, along the corridor, and off through the house, which he left inside another half-hour. He went to join the throng of the City, the religious processions, the hucksters, players, taverns.

It was as if he had been reprieved from a severe sentence, but this did not occur to him.

There was a summer storm, the sky the colour of cinders, and the rain falling in remote leaden drops. In the tavern called the *Surprise*, Joseph tapped Raoulin's shoulder, and Raoulin, turning with some pleasure to pick up their friendship, was only surprised when Joseph said, straight out like a cough or swear word: 'That girl's dead.'

The sentence shocked in several ways. Raoulin could not sort them.

'Eh? Which girl?' he blurted.

'The little blonde harlot. Shall I say how?' Joseph's spectacles enlarged his eyes like two monstrous tears.

'How then?'

Joseph sighed. 'She filled a bladder with some corrosive tincture and squirted it up inside herself.'

There was a nothingness then, rather than a silence, between them, while the normal racket of the *Surprise* went on all about. At last Raoulin murmured, 'How did she come by such a thing?'

'Oh, there is a physician for the girls. He practises with the alchemical arts and keeps a cupboard of ointments and mixtures. She visited him on a pretext, and stole the essence. It may be she didn't understand its strength . . . They heard her cries but couldn't save her. A ghastly death.'

Raoulin had turned deathly sick, as though he himself had been poisoned. His genitals burned. The room trembled as is under water. 'And do you blame *me* for this?'

'No! Blame you? No. And yet.'

To his absolute confusion, Raoulin felt the pressure of grief mounting up his senses into his eyes like a wave. He rose suddenly, pushing away from the bench, thrusting by Joseph as if he hated him – he did hate him and was sure the sentiment was shared – and got out into the alley by the wine-shop. Here, leaning on the masonry, he vomited his drink. Good. *Good.* He should suffer some penance. Where to run? Into a church? Oh *God* – what had she reckoned, that stupid little trull, with her sweet face and silly mouth, and eyes wise to everything except what she would work on herself.

He had not even now been able to vomit away the question – *Why*? or the cause – *himself*.

It was a truth, he had been spared much distress. He was young, and lucky. Death and illness, misery and want, the ancient degree of panic itself, were matters apart from Raoulin. He had read of states and afflictions, in books. But until this hour the wing of night had not brushed him. Scratched by its metallic feathers, he quailed.

The lead sky leaned on Paradys. Her heights pressed up against it in luminescent stabs. Still the whole impact of the thunder and the rain was not released.

He beheld above him the cliffs of the Temple-Church. He had gone over much ground, had crossed the river, without seeing. A cruel olivine glare glittered on the holy windows. The processions were done. Christ had gone in again and left the world to sin and savagery, and to all the inexplicable shades.

Raoulin stood a minute on that runnel of path nicknamed, by some, "Satan's Way", and did not know it.

Then continued his dreary ascent towards the house called d'Uscaret.

The storm broke loose on the City at midnight, and roused several thousand sleepers, of whom Raoulin was only one.

His last thoughts had been of a childish running away. He had wanted to leave it all, the City, the university, the fever of learning, to escape back into the dull safe farm where nothing bad had ever happened to him, or been told to him in any way he had to credit.

But waking at the blast of the thunder and the shattering rain flung through the windows, he knew at once what he must do instead.

There was after all one here in this house who could tell him what had made the name of d'Uscaret so vile it killed.

Raoulin got up and secured the shutters of his two rooms. He had slept in his clothes and now tidied himself, and drank the ale left with his untouched supper.

Then, with two candles lit on the branch, and his knife in his belt, he took himself from the chamber and went to seek the recluse in her tower. No longer in the spirit of romance or unchastity. But with a grim purpose; as a right.

On the stair to the upper corridor, something checked him. He had the thought to put out the candles. Thunder bellowed and the stone-work seemed to whine. What use two feeble flames? He quenched them. And then, entering the corridor there was candleshine enough soaking out from the hidden chamber, whose door was standing wide. A figure came from it, slender, high-waisted, *hers*.

The light she carried dipped, swooped up and formed an arch, a funnel. The dark centre of the light, she flowed away and seemed drawn down into the earth – she was descending the stair towards the garden.

With the stealth of a starving hunter, Raoulin followed.

From the stair-head he glimpsed her below, a spectral creature still, on the threshold of the garden and the tempest. Then with one blow the howling night quaffed her candle. A rushing filled the doorway – rain and noise. She was gone into the weather.

On the edge of night, his civilised self held him back half a moment. Then he too was plunged in wet and chaos.

The water gushed upon his head and shoulders. It beat him, and slapped his face over and over, and he could not see.

On all sides the trees of the garden groaned and foamed like rivers.

The quick-growing weeds which, if trodden down and broken, in a day or night of fecund summer would reweave themselves, had formerly concealed any other excursions through the garden. It had seemed unvisited for years. But perhaps she walked here often, under sun and moon, under downpour, in the winter snow –

He had continued forcing himself forward through the night, and now he glimpsed the great yew ahead, where the mausoleum gaped from the foliage, the little house of Helise the dead bride.

The rain all at once slackened, and was lifted up like a swag of heavy curtaining. He heard the fountain breath of the drenched trees, and the individual notes of oval glass beads falling from branch to branch. The moon struck suddenly from a cloud like a spear. In the entry of the tomb stood a woman in a black gown, with dead-white hands clasped upon a dead candle, a white stalk of throat and a white face in a powdery bloom of hair.

In those instants she was uncanny, the dead one risen from her grave.

Because of this, he could not make himself move or speak.

And then, the shadowy features of her face (like the smudged shadows on the face of the moon itself) realigned themselves. It was she who spoke to him.

'Who are you? What do you want?'

A fundamental inquiry, perhaps a fearful one, given the time and place, and since she was not a phantom.

Raoulin took some random steps nearer. There was no explanation he could offer that would in any way humanly excuse his action.

Thus he said, 'And you, lady, why did you come here in the rain?'

She leaned out of the porch of the tomb at him, her face tilted upward. He saw it was the face of the dream and that, even in the moon's colourless ray, the discs of her eyes, lent only a hint of proper light, would flood with greenness, like the trees.

'Who are you?' she said again.

'My name is Raoulin,' he said, wondering if she had been told of him. That must be so. For she had come seeking him that first night, and stared into his sleep when he dreamed. 'And you, demoiselle?' he added, for it appeared she was young, after all the speculation, and yet, being moon-like, ageless and old, under her surfaces.

'I?' she said. 'Who am I?' She lowered her lunar-emerald eyes. 'You may read my name above me.'

He looked irresistibly above her head, and there on the stone banner ran the letters, as he had seen before: *Helise d'Uscaret.*

'A namesake of the dead girl,' he said.

'Oh no. This tomb is mine, which naturally is why I visit here. I'm long dead, Sieur Raoulin. And therefore why should a storm deter me?'

For all her reality, her body, her shadow going away from her on the path, again the skin crawled over his bones.

Harshly he said, 'The rain wets your gown. You drink wine from a glass and need a candle in the dark.'

'Do I? You mean to say I'm flesh and blood. Yes. But yet, I died. I died and was awarded this black box. I went down to the court of death as they so prettily describe it, or

27

so I take the Latin to mean, and perhaps I decipher wrongly. You are the scholar, Sieur Raoulin. Do I have the message right?'

He said, 'You questioned the old woman about me.'

Then she smiled.

'It's been many years,' she replied, 'since there was any life in the house. And suddenly, a young man from the provinces. I confess the fault of curiosity.'

'Do you confess, too, stealing into the room and watching me as I slept?'

'You are unchivalrous, sieur. Asking that I admit such a thing.'

'The dead can't expect much courtesy,' he answered boldly.

Her glancing conversation irked, but also flattered him. She was very beautiful. It was very strange.

'Perhaps,' she said then, 'perhaps I shall resolve this riddle for you. If you have the will and wish to listen.'

'What else,' he said.

Her eyes fixed upon his. Even in the darkness now he saw that they were green.

'You may not believe the story I tell you. It's incredible and utterly exact. I can't lie. That is my – atonement.'

'I'm all impatience,' he said.

'Then, I invite you to my chamber. With me, no codes of propriety remain, to be upheld or sullied. As you say, the dead can hope for slight courtesy.'

'I won't harm you,' he said.

She smiled again. 'Don't trouble. It's understood.'

She went before him through the garden, the skirts of her gown brushing off rain-opals from the bushes. Such jewels were strewn in her hair, grey gems in a white web, for she wore it quite loosely, carelessly.

He followed her back into the house and up the stair. His pulses beat, insisting on carnal matters; but his brain stayed wholly clear. It was not for a tryst he companioned this one.

The room that she led him into was unlike the rest of the

house. Eight candles burned and lit a painted floor of squares, and showed the ceiling too was figured with scrolls and smouldery fruit. The posted bed stood partially away behind a curtain, and guarded by a chest of carved ebony. There was the window, to glow its marsh-light on the City. There, a broad fireplace bordered by columns, with a pale fire frisking in it. This, after the rain, was solacing. Two black chairs, with footstools, faced each other across the hearth, a table between with a book upon it, and also a silver pitcher and two glass goblets of the valuable kind he had seen before.

He could not fail to be aware this room had some resemblance to the make-believe bedroom at the brothel. Or that it too had been prepared for a guest. Madly it came to him that everything that had gone on, since his first entry to the City, was in the nature of a dance-measure, and none of it quite real, or what it seemed.

'Be seated,' said Helise d'Uscaret, if so she was, and why should she not be so?

He obeyed her, taking the right-hand chair.

In the window-embrasure, another book lay, and a little casket. Here and there were scattered small tokens of life, of femininity – a hand-mirror of polished metal, a ribbon, a flaxen bud in a thimble of water. (Nowhere, that he could see, a skull.) Charmingly, from under the bed-curtain, a satin slipper peeped out.

And like the attitude of the table and two chairs, these items had an air of considered arrangement.

Into his glass she poured a dark wine.

He caught the scent of it, and of her, as she bent over him and drew away. Certainly, she was a living woman.

Beauty. Strangeness.

She seated herself in the opposing chair, and sipped from her own glass a vintage like ink. But now he could see the impossible colour of her gaze.

'Be at ease,' she said.

'Your eyes,' he said, as if he could not prevent himself, 'never in the world – so *green*.'

'Long ago,' she said, 'my eyes were not green at all. That is the badge of what befell me. The mark on me. My eyes are my scar, after the battle.'

It seemed to Raoulin he would not move now, not even to raise the fine glass to his lips. This stasis did not distress him. His mind was alert, to be instructed. Nothing else was of importance.

PART TWO

The Bride

And what will ye wear for your wedding lace?
　　One with another.
A heavy heart and a hidden face,
　　Mother, my mother.

Swinburne

A girl is grown like a flower in the house of her kindred. She is nurtured for her hues and perfume. At the blossoming she will be plucked from her native soil and planted elsewhere. In other earth she will give fruit, fade, wither, and finish. This is all the usefulness of such a flower, the well-born girl among the great houses of Paradys.

Helise la Valle knew, as she had learnt her alphabet and orisons, that this was her destiny.

Indeed, she had looked forward to the event of her transplanting, once she became conscious of the future. Rather than be afraid, it seemed to her child-mind like the festival of Christmas or the New Year, a season of celebration, dressing-up, the giving and receiving of gifts. Late to these images came a dreamlike icon: the bridegroom.

It was not until her adolescence, actually her saint's day, in her twelfth year, that this procrastinate shape at last stepped forward to overwhelm, to *crush* all the others, and fill her with pervasive dread.

On that day it was that she heard his name for the first time. What is named, in the oldest rituals of witchcraft, takes power.

'Heros d'Uscaret,' sang out the youngest cousin.

31

And at this, all the elder cousins fell entirely silent, as if a wind had passed over that robbed them of speech and motion.

'Who is he?' asked Helise.

She was a fey girl, whose quiet attentiveness led adults to think her docile. She had never been discouraged in asking questions, for she asked so few.

'You're to be wed to him,' said one of the elder cousins, looking abashed, for propriety had been breached. 'You are betrothed.'

'Am I?' said Helise, merely interested.'

But just then one of the most senior cousins came briskly into the room, clapping her hands and frowning.

The maidens were disbanded. Only the Name was left.

It was at the hour of candle-lighting that Helise approached her mother.

'I am to marry Heros – d'Usc – d'Uscaret?'

The mother started. She was seated in her chair before a glowing hearth (it was autumn, and the nights already were cold) idly combing the long hair of her little lap-dog. At its mistress' start, the tiny animal growled. Helise did not like the dog, for it had once bitten her with its sharp rat teeth. She blamed the dog for this, and not the sickly cosseting and ill-temper of her own mother, which had formed it.

'What did you say, Helise?'

'That I'm to marry – am betrothed – '

'Very well,' said the mother. 'You are. It's a distinguished match.'

Helise stood between excitement and disarray. She had always known her life would alter, but here was sudden proof.

'Heros,' she said again, 'd'Uscar – et.'

'Someone has been twittering,' said the mother. Her sallow proud face was unkind. 'Your cousins.'

'But Mother, mustn't I know?'

'In good time. You mayn't wed tomorrow. It will be three

good years before you are fit. Your father is strict.'
  'But shall I know nothing of it?'
  'The suitor is young enough, twenty years when you are
fifteen. Sound, not a cripple. Fair, I have heard. His house
is of the best. They've the favour of the Duke.'
  Helise, at twelve, had already been in love, with a painting of Jehanus the Baptist on the Martyr Chapel wall of the
Sacrifice. She understood that it was futile to love a saint in
such a manner. But since her own sensuality was to herself
undivulged, she did not perceive it for what it was, and had
never realised she sinned in her wild thoughts. In her head
she pictured to herself the court of Herod, where she saved
the saint from death (thereby depriving him, of course, of
his martyrdom, maybe of his sainthood) and the clutches of
Herod, shameless Salomé, and the Romans. She accom-
panied Jehanus into the desert where, respected among his
followers, she wove him garlands from the locust tree, tended
him in sickness, swooned and revived in his miraculous
embrace, and, in the river to her breasts, was baptised by
the fiery water spilling from his hands. The face of Jehanus
in the fresco, formed by an artist of genius, had often
become the subject for some young girl's fantasy. The arched
throat, mane of hair, and great upraised eyes, were tautly
luminous with that agony of suffering or joy inherent in
worldly pain. Or pleasure. Kept ignorant, the perceptive in-
stincts of Helise had already been a trifle warped.
  It was her whimsy perhaps that Heros d'Uscaret, described,
should resemble her first love.
  But the Lady la Valle would not describe Heros d'Uscaret.
  It took a maid in the closeted bedroom to do that.
  She was crying, this girl, only a year or so older than her
mistress. Helise, having been well-educated in many alternative
areas, beat her maid's hands with an ivory comb, to come at the
cause.
  'Oh madam – they've promised you to a monster!'
  'What do you mean?' said Helise.

'There's a curse on that house.'

The maid snivelled, and Helise raked her again with the comb.

'Madam – Satan claims all the men of their line – and the women. But the men are – shape-changers – they are *things under the skin.*'

At this nonsensical, beastly phrase, Helise left off her interrogation. Her immature mind had now quite enough to play upon.

For five days she was in a fever and the physicians despaired of her life. Then she recovered, and they congratulated their own skills.

The talk of betrothal and terror seemed sloughed with illness. It was not referred to. Helise resumed her former habit, and never asked.

(The maid was gone. There was a new maid, a country girl who was not acquainted with the City.)

What one does not speak of need not be believed.

So Helise continued until her fifteenth year, near the end of which they informed her that, soon after her birthday, she was to wed a noble lord of the City, whose name had already been made known to her. By then she had all but forgotten the awful words, her fever dreams. Therefore the icy hand that gripped her heart seemed to have no source.

In the assembled months before her wedding-day, Helise was wan and languid. Her mother and aunts chided her. She would lose her good looks and demean her house. She must eat this and drink that, she must have these unctions applied to her skin and those pastes to her hair.

At fifteen, Helise had mostly dispensed with questions. Her native indifference to the outer world was augmented by realisation that what might be answered was invariably told without inquiry – and what would not be answered would not.

At night in her narrow virgin's bed, Helise offered vague prayers to a fate that was unavoidable; she prayed as a man prays to be spared death. Perhaps delay was possible.

But the months clambered over each other and the wedding-day came hurrying nearer. The bride was not afforded a single glimpse of the groom.

A priest came to instruct Helise, a man elderly and superlatively uncomely, as was thought correct in the case of a young girl.

One morning, as they sat in the la Valle vine court, Helise spoke to the priest.

'My betrothed is Lord Heros, the heir of House d'Uscaret.' It was not a question, nor did the priest reply. Until now he had somehow managed not to name the name of the bridegroom, though referring to him always deferentially. 'Spiritual father,' said Helise, looking only at her knotted hands, 'when I was a child, I was frightened by tales of evil that had to do with – '

'This isn't the hour to dwell on such foolishness,' said the priest. 'You must think only of your duties as a wife. Be wary, my daughter, that you don't interpose such nasty and aimless chatter.'

'But spiritual father, these tales concerned my husband.'

The priest looked as steadily upon the vines as Helise upon her hands. Neither met the other's eye.

'Put superstition from your mind, my daughter.'

'But father – I'm afraid.'

The priest inhaled and expelled a noisy breath laden with garlic and kitchen wine. He said, 'There have been stories told of d'Uscaret, by the ignorant and stupid, notions instigated by enemies of that valiant house.' Then he paused, as if girding himself, and added, 'What have you heard?'

Helise stammered that she could recall no details.

At that, the priest seemed happier.

'If you can remember no absolute, how can you fear?'

Helise attempted to confide that she did not know, yet fear persisted.

But the priest would have none of that. He rebuked her with sins of self-attention and untrust. Would her loving parents give her over to any tainted man? And did she not have faith in her God to protect her?

Helise sat quiescent under this garlicky lesson, until he left off and went on with the others.

It appeared to her that all with whom she now had dealings, all that were caught up in the train of the approaching marriage, adopted an odd manner. Faces she had been familiar with now looked like masks, and voices did not run along but went choppily, with words left unsaid. And how often she saw the hands rising and falling upon the breasts, marking there a cross. Did the maids stare nervously sideways at her, as if at one who may be infected with plague? Did her aunt's singing bird go dumb in its cage at her passing?

The shadow is on me. Am I going to die?

She knew nothing of the real rites of marriage, nothing of sex beyond the untutored flarings of her own body, which she had obliquely discovered by then were dangerous, as they might lead her into unchastity. Connubiality was this: the husband lay beside his wife all night in the same bed. Sometimes (so certain cousins had assured her) he kissed his wife, even her nakedness, and some men, though surely they were depraved, set their hands on a woman's private places. Helise had never even seen cats mating. Though once she had beheld a cat in labour, and was appalled. Later on, hearing her brother's wife shrieking in childbirth, Helise had had some idea why. The angels of God brought the baby. It was God's will, and His will also that a woman suffer in travail, the female penance for the disobedience of Eve.

Could it be that Heros d'Uscaret would perpetrate on his bride some alarming foul act, something worse even than the embarrassing things that apparently quite normally went on, these lewd kissings and touchings already mentioned.

Ten nights before her wedding-night, Helise recalled precisely what her maid had said to her: 'Satan claims them – shape-changers – *things under the skin.*'

She woke in a bath of sweat, and bit her hands with terror.

Paradys turned out to recognise the wedding processions of the houses la Valle and d'Uscaret, and to catch the sweetmeats and small money retainers might throw the rabble. They were able to watch besides many scores of men on fine horses, dazzling in brocade and gems, some quantities of damsels clothed like graces and strewing petals, musicians with lutes and shawms, and pages with banners.

The bride rode on a dappled palfrey with a headstall of pearls. The girl's dress was of cloth-of-silver, with under-sleeves of cream silk stitched with brilliants. Her blonde hair fluttered loose but for a jewelled cap of silver daisies and sea-green peridots. Her face was white, but there was nothing uncommon in that.

The bridegroom's family cantered up, heavy with their colours of sable and viridian. The sigil of d'Uscaret was a cruel preying bird, perhaps a falcon. They were a wealthy house, and bullion clanked on everything, and in the jaunty hat of the young groom was a diamond said to have been dug from the forehead of a dragon in the Holy Land . . . Otherwise, the hat, the light, the shade, hid the young man's face, though he cut a brave enough figure. His locks were blonder even than those of the little white bride.

Helise found herself entering the Temple-Church, and acknowledged that the astonishing horror had arrived, was here, about to happen to her.

From the moment of her waking at dawn, through all the preparation of her person, somehow *she* had gone far off. They had bathed and anointed her and clad her in the silver gown – but she had been at a distance, hanging in the air.

As her body rode along the route on the demure palfrey, the wedding music in its ears, the finery flashing at its eyes like drawn knives, her soul was in a trance.

But now the wanderer had returned, was trapped and must participate. There was to be no escape.

The grey pillars of the Temple-Church rose like tree-trunks of a petrified forest. The roof was ribbed – the inner belly of some apocryphal beast which had swallowed the processions whole. Rays of daylight pierced through. From a massive window a bolt of sunshine streamed and smoked.

An angel of white marble shone out in the path, but did not save Helise. Beyond, the Angel Chapel was an underwater cave where she would drown in marriage.

And now she was at the rail, and now she was alone but for one who stood beside her.

It seemed to her that no one else at all was there.

No maids-of-honour, no gentlemen, no witnesses, not even the priest. Not even her parents, who had condemned her.

Only this other at her side.

Something – the priest's injunction – brought them to kneel.

Helise knelt, and her gown rustled and the small jewels clinked against the tessellated floor. And she heard the scuff of a shoe, the brushing of a viridian sleeve.

The blessing was being spoken, the magical water was being sprinkled. Could a devil endure that? Seemingly yes, for he had not sprung aside, his garments did not singe.

The responses of the Mass drew from her a whisper. At her side a male voice murmured low its clear Latin. A young male voice, younger than the voices of her father and brother.

Surely, a demon could not utter the responses of God's Mass?

The one beside her had a voice, and now a hand, resting

upon the rail. The hand stayed Helise, for it was in shape the hand of a warrior-saint, made thin and strong for the hilt of battle, the clasp of prayer. And on the fourth finger, an onyx ring.

The priest, having changed the wafers to the flesh and the wine to the ichor of Christ, fed them at the rail like two hungry sparrows.

But could a demon take between its lips the body and blood of Heaven?

Now she must stand up again. She must make the correct replies to the questions of the priest. Like all questions, in her experience, the answers were preordained, unavoidable. Only questions that might be answered could ever be asked.

And so, in a few minutes more, she had been wedded, and had barely noticed, puzzling as she was over the paradox of the pale hand with the onyx, and the Host penetrating the intestines of one accursed.

Finally the pale hand itself took her own and on to her finger ran a coil of cold metal, to bind her, and the priest in turn bound her right hand to the pale hand. Tied, she must turn. Or, *they* turned her.

Handfast, Helise looked at her bridegroom, her husband. There before her, straight and slender, his face in a halo of un-coloured hair, was Jehanus, the beautiful, harrowed martyr from off the very wall. Only his eyes were altered. Their beauty had been brought to life with a green and stellar fire.

Bound fast hand-to-hand with her, he kissed her passion-lessly with his cool mouth. It was a fearsome kiss, for it struck Helise in the breast and heart, into her womb even, down to the soles of her feet, like lightning. As in the Bible, a sword had gone through her. She had never known before what that phrase could mean.

Outside, the crowd shouted. She was put again on to the palfrey. They went up through the City, up to the mansion of d'Uscaret. And sometimes the thrown flowers smote Helise, and some wisps of paper, one of which lodged in her sleeve, and looking at it she saw it was a votive prayer for her safety. But now she did not mind. He rode at her side.

The viridian banners by the doors were garlanded with myrtle. This house was black, like a sarcophagus, and the great hall was black, with old charred flags like broken wings drooping from the rafters. But the candles burned and white damask clothed the tables and he led her to sit beside him.

Helise was happy. Her eyes sparkled and everything had become wonderful. They gave her white wine to drink, and on the gallery minstrels sang like angels.

They banqueted on fowl roasted with figs and cakes of flour and sugar, milk jellies, fish served in their armour, doves in their feathers. There were salads of spinach and beans made into gardens, and castles of rice and pine kernels, and almond puddings sweet as the promise of life everlasting.

A pageant was performed, displaying the prowess of d'Uscaret, her knights and lords, their deeds of valour.

Lilies fell from a canopy.

At the table sat the new father and mother of Helise. He was a dark and peevish man, fretful, who drank until huge drops spurred out on his forehead. The woman was like something cut from wood, having only two dimensions, angular in her tourmaline gown, her silver caul and steeple headdress from which black spiderspun floated.

What did they matter?

At the side of Helise sat Jehanus who was Heros, still and nearly silent, real as all things, given to her by God.

I am his wife, and he is –

He was beautiful as a young divinity. Had she suffered so only to be intoxicated by this ecstasy?

The masque in the hall was now of a girl and youth embraced upon an isle on wheels, while tame panthers frisked about – but they were all men inside the feline velvets. A dim cry floated on the sea of delight: *shape-changer*.

'Come, madam. Now, lady, come with us – '

D'Uscaret's maids of honour, the young girls of the
house, were urging her bashfully, wantonly. She must get
up and go with them, to the bridal chamber.

Helise rose and let them lead her out. Their butterfly mut-
ters and touches, playful, childishly-naughty, swirling her
through a door and up an inner stair where brands blazed
in brackets. A vast heat was on the stair, bringing out the
scents of flesh and unguents, and above in the curve of a
shadow, the arch, the corridor, great doors carved with
falcons, through which they slipped like thieves. And there
the room, the room, and the tall wide bed, where tonight she
would lie beside her lord.

Now she could reconcile herself with all of it. Yes, she
could conjure endless darkness furled in ceaseless embrace.
His mouth on hers, his arms about her. And if he should
wish more – whatever he wished she would grant.

The girls of d'Uscaret, with sighings and nonsensical acid
ribaldries – traditional things they probably did not, all of
them, comprehend – disrobed Helise and clad her in a shift
of samite, combed out her hair and wove lilies in it. She
climbed into the high bed, and they arranged her there like
a toy, leaning on the pillows.

At the hour of Matines, the wedding-party bounded up
the stair with torches and candles, bells and lyres, bringing
the husband to his wife.

The solid doors flew wide, and between them the uproar
surged, the lights and sequins and the blowing of tin
trumpets. The old men making sour old dirty jests, and the
women laughing or compressing their faces. The Lady
d'Uscaret was there, like a pillar of flint. Her perspectiveless
face also contorted to smile or grimace, but it was like a disc
of paper.

Before all the horde, the bridegroom. He made the rest
into a dumbshow.

They brought him forward to the bed, and the men instructed him and the women looked away.

The eldest of the maids of honour bowed.

'Your bride is here awaiting you, m'sire. May you have joy of your night.'

Then, hiding their faces coyly, the maids ran away, and the old men tried to catch them going down the stairs, so there were shrieks and a scattering of sugarplums.

With a susurrus of trains and mantles, the doorway sucked back the last of the crowd. The doors were shut.

Heros and Helise, alone now, in the bedchamber.

She sat in the bed, as if in a bank of snow. She knew she must be shy like the gentle female deer. Her heart drummed, and she watched him under her lids.

What would he do now? She did not care, so long as he would lie down with her. She was parched for his nearness, the pressure of his mouth and body. This was true lust she felt, and did not even know it.

But Heros went straight back to the doors, and in came one of his gentlemen. Behind a screen painted with a hunting or hawking scene, the bridegroom was undressed. He stepped out from the screen wrapped in a mantle, and the gentleman took himself away, and again the door was shut.

And now, now surely, Heros would come to her.

But, as if he were alone only with himself, Heros d'Uscaret wandered along the length and breadth of the chamber. He seemed deep in thought. Now and then he hesitated, picking up some article or other. Once he stood for several minutes reading at an open book on a stand.

Helise did not dare to call to him. To question.

Her suspense became firstly painful, and then sickening, as gradually her trembling warmth died into chill.

As though he perceived this, Heros circled once more and snuffed the candles.

A veil of blackness covered the chamber, edge-to-edge, shrinking it to the area of the bed, where one light remained burning on the chest at the bedfoot.

Heros now moved towards this final candle, it enamelled him upon the dark.

There and then, he looked at his wife.

Before she could control herself, she leaned from the pillows, as if to hold out her arms to him.

But Heros d'Uscaret, her husband, blew out the candle. And as she shivered there, he got in beside her, and reclined, with the space of a third person left between them. And he said, 'Goodnight, Helise.'

Perhaps only minutes later, lying beside and apart from him, she whispered, 'Have I offended you, my lord?'

'No,' said the darkness.

'But will you not then – ' and here she faltered on her own unspeakable audacity.

After her anguish had gone on for some minutes more, Helise stretched herself out, and visualised that now they lay together as man and wife should. But her instinct knew perfectly well that this was not as it should be. Blindly, her instinct clawed at the night while she kept like a stone, but after a century had passed, she murmured, 'But will you not – kiss me, my lord?'

This question was answered.

'No,' darkness said again. 'I won't do that.'

And then there went by aeons of blackness and heartbeats like massing tides in the shell of the ear. After which Heros d'Uscaret said, 'In the morning, Helise, you must take a pin and make your finger bleed. Stain the sheet with it, and your shift. That's for the showing, to prove your virginity is gone. Without that your life will be miserable here. More miserable than necessary. Do you understand?'

She did not, of course. Of course she said that she did.

There were a hundred things – she did not know how they must be expressed. She lay in black silence, until he added, 'Go to sleep now.' And then she lay awake all night until the dawn.

*

'Well, demoiselle. Do you please my son?'

Helise, a bride of eight days, gazed modestly on the ground. Eventually she found some words. 'I try to, madam.'

'Come, lift your head. I can tell a liar by his eyes.'

Helise lifted her head, but not her gaze.

'Look up,' said the implacable Lady d'Uscaret.

Helise looked up. Just like her other mother, this one in her inlaid chair, but having no lap-dog.

The eyes of the second mother were black. Her dark hair was imprisoned within a birdcage of silver-wire, with a band of nacre across her pallid forehead. Everything was hardness, even the folds of her gown seemed hacked from steel.

'You're afraid of me, Helise,' pronounced d'Uscaret's lady. 'But that's as it should be. Your family's rich, but has no history, in comparison with this house. Beside my own lineage, your name is a title written in sand.' Helise might have been surprised; already, not interpreting, she had seen that the new mother despised her own husband. But the new mother continued. 'I too am by birth a d'Uscaret. But of the elder line. *We* may trace our roots to the days of the emperors at Rome. My lord is of the lesser branch. My blood kin are dead. A plague . . .' She paused, her eyes not softened but made adamant by memory or bitterness. 'Perhaps you've heard legends of the d'Uscaret? These concern *my* kindred.' (Helise could not ascertain if this boast concerned legends of might, or myths of – other things.) 'I alone am left. And my son. My son is d'Uscaret. He has the sign on him. His fairness. His wonderful eyes. Once, my own eyes . . . Do you love my son?' said the Lady of d'Uscaret as if she spoke of dross.

Helise bowed her head again.

'Madam, yes.'

'Naturally. How could it be otherwise. But to you he is indifferent. Am I correct?'

Helise wavered between shame and fright.

'Oh,' said the hard woman, as she would flick a fly from her gown, 'you are serviceable. You may entertain his nights and bear him a boy or two. But that's all. His brood-mare.'

Helise stared at the flags as if at the gate of Hades.

'Poor little mite,' said Lady d'Uscaret, without compassion. 'At least you have the wit to know he is a god, and far above you. You won't annoy him, I believe. Never do that. It was a marriage of convenience. You brought cash, and we thank you, Helise. Remember your place here. You are a pretty beetle we keep to amuse us now and then.' She leaned her snake's head thoughtfully upon her bone hand. 'Go away.'

And Helise gathered up her skirts and hastened from the room.

The world was as it always had been, incomprehensible, unyielding. She had her part. A lesser part perhaps, here. She had fundamentally as much sway over the house as had her brother's wife at la Valle. If she was dutiful, and did not thwart them, they would not chastise her.

The humble were the elect of God. Did not the priests teach so, in their gemmed, kingly robes, from their towering pulpits.

Helise spent her days in ladylike domestic forms. She embroidered, she pressed flowers. She had no talent for music, and reading soon tired her. At the proper times she heard Mass with the household in the family chapel. Food might have been a diversion but she had no appetite.

At dinner, sometimes she saw her husband.

Generally the great ancestral hall was not employed, d'Uscaret dined in a parlour of panelled walls, where were displayed some paintings on classical and religious subjects. Above the table, whose legs were in the shape of eagles, three silver herb-censers depended from the ceiling, with aromatics burning over charcoal, to perfume the air. All d'Uscaret that was present in the house assembled here, in this show-place, with their house dogs lying at their feet, and the tame monkey of the lord's brother eating candied cucumber or running about the length of its leash.

If he should be there, Heros was seated beside Helise. But sometimes he had gone hawking, beyond Paradys, or to some library, or cloister, or to another house. Sometimes father, uncle, and son were all of them absent, at the Duke's table.

She seldom saw her lord during the day in any case. As, by then, she saw him seldom at night.

The first month he did spend with her, prostrate every night at her side. She would lie sleepless most of the hours, tortured by nervous cramps, afraid to be restless. Hearing the level breathing of his sleep, the dim bells of Matines and Laude, sometimes the reborn bell of Prima Hora. If she ever fell asleep it would be towards the dawn, and waking when the sky was light, she would see he had already left her.

She had stained the sheet as he had told her to, that initial morning, with the blood of her finger. She had had to force herself to prick her skin with the point, for she was, that way, a coward. She did it to content Heros, ignorant as to why. Were they then supposed to have acted out together some rite of viciousness and tearing, to cause blood. Was she fortunate to have been spared?

After one month, he did not come to sleep by her often, maybe every eight or ten days. Foolishly, when he entered the room, and when his gentleman unclothed him behind the screen, Helise hoped – but did not know for what. For a kiss, an embrace?

He gave her nothing, no more than in the beginning. Usually he would bid her goodnight, as he would greet her when he met her at dinner. They exchanged few other words, and at night none at all.

In the third month of her life at d'Uscaret, an elderly woman of the house came to Helise in the small square chamber allocated her sitting-room, that lay off the blank bed-chamber.

The woman was bustling and beady-eyed. She seemed respected in the house, and sat at dinner with the family. Her position Helise had never been certain of, but had once or twice heard her referred to. 'Consult Ysanne if you still have your cough.' Or, 'Hush, that's a matter for old Ysanne.'

Now the old woman, who was fat, and wrapped her head in an Eastern turban of silk, sat across the fireless hearth and watched Helise, until the young girl turned hot and cold together.

'Have you noticed anything?' said old Ysanne at length, in a gossipy tone.

Helise could only look.

'Come, come,' said Ysanne. 'Speak out. Do you vomit in the morning, or at certain foods? Have your courses stopped or grown erratic?'

Helise suddenly became aware that sickness and the stoppage of blood implied a gift of pregnancy.

She shook her head. Here was another failing. And yet (she had randomly grasped enough) she suspected the fault was not all her own. There was something which occurred between the husband and the wife, in bed, some sorcerous communion or vow, which invoked children.

Ysanne now got up again, and said, 'You know you must give your husband an heir?' Helise did not reply. What could she say? 'Timid,' said Ysanne. 'The young wife must overcome her blushes and cherish her lord. You mustn't shrink from anything he wishes.'

Helise felt faint. It was terrified lust, although she did not know it.

After a litter of more meaningless admonishments, old Ysanne went flat-footedly out.

Helise, as she had not done before, broke into sobs and

47

tears. She even prayed, although she had long accepted God did not listen. Who else was there to talk to?

Then, in her abject wretchedness, when she could think of no shelter and no friend whose counsel she might seek, piercing her like the awl, her inner heart told her what she should do. She must run to *him*, to the one who never spoke to her, who never or rarely lay beside her, to he who was the cause of all her hurt, for he was also her love, the reason she had lived at all.

The decision of unthinking love was an insanity and it made her bold, perhaps for the first time in her existence.

She left her futile stitchery, and walked slowly, as if with an invited purpose, up through the house.

She had begun to learn its thoroughfares almost by default. She knew the situation of that other room, in which her lord slept, when not with his wife. She must go northerly, towards the most ancient portion of the building. She passed servants, but none challenged her. To them, she was a lady, a facet of d'Uscaret, however slight. Long corridors lit by windows, hung with tapestry, and quartered with carven benches, gave on thinner darker lanes, whose windows had no glass but only bars, whose occasional tapestries rotted. No longer did any servants appear. There was a dull silence. Yet she did not lose her way. For in the wilderness there was still some sign of habitation, or passage. Here and there a landmark of a great chest, even the mossy blackened hangings — for elsewhere the corridors were closed by grilles of spiderweb, the floors seas of dust — empty of anything human, limitlessly undisturbed.

So she found her way to a twisting stair she had once or twice heard described. It was the path into the tower-top, the Bird Tower they called it: doves had been kept there once. Now Heros dwelled in the apartment, as if upon a rock in that desert of wasted corridors and rooms.

The door was abruptly above her. On its timber, a falcon's mask in iron, and an iron ring.

As she put her hand on it she realised the door would be locked fast. She would have to sit down under the door-sill and await his return.

But the door gave at a pressure on the ring, without even a resistance.

That frightened her. She saw at once all her temerity in daring to invade the sanctum where no servant, no kindred, would enter unasked.

Yet it was too late, for the chamber opened before her, all its mystery, its spell, for it was his.

She stepped straight off the stair into the room.

It seemed to her the cell of a scholar. The bed was narrow and low, with a footstool by it, and a plain chest. No evidence of luxury was in these things. But across the floor, beneath a high, round, glassed window, that showed only air, was a table laid with a feast of objects and books, with measures and globes, the bones of hideous creatures mounted up as if they lived, weird instruments of alchemy and science.

There, on that board, his interest and his commitment were spread. She knew immediately, and with the jealous pang of a rival.

Between the table and the wall a three-paned triptych had been raised upon a stand.

Peering over the items on the table, careful to dislodge nothing, Helise did not pay the painting much attention. But then something in the angle of it, catching the window light against the shadow of the wall, caught her eye. It was his, of his choosing. She went to see.

How strange then, these images after all, strange as anything maybe in the room, or stranger . . .

In the first painted panel was a fang-like mountain side parting a ravenous sky. A procession of men and women had ascended, with livid torches; they stood like mindless things, staring into the clouds. Something with black wings was carrying off a young girl in white. From her lolling limbs and head there streamed draperies and hair, and a wreath of flowers went tumbling earthwards. This ominous tableau was titled in gilt: *Nuptiae*.

In the second panel, the scene was a bedchamber by night, a vast couch where something lay asleep. In the foreground, holding back the curtains with one hand, and tilting in the other an antique, flaming lamp, a pale girl leaned forward, her slenderness rigid in lines of anxiety and expectation, endeavouring to see –

This picture was labelled: *Noli me spectare*.

Helise knew now what the triptych portrayed. It was the legend of Cupido and Psyche. The maiden had been left as a sacrifice for a demon, and was accordingly carried off. In a mountain mansion, cared for by invisible sprites, the girl was visited in deepest darkness by one who claimed to be her husband and lord. He was to her only the best of lovers, but warned her in the blindfold black: *Never attempt to look on me*.

(Hence the two titles – *Nuptiae*, an ironical ''marriage'', and the second, perhaps perversely mimicking the instruction of Christ: *'See me not.'*)

But Psyche had been persuaded by desire and doubt to forget this ban. When he slept she lit a lamp, and so beheld her spouse. He was the god of love himself, handsome and perfect. And in her amazement, her shaking hand let drop a scorch of oil upon his shoulder. He woke, he disowned her, and into the unkind world she was cast out lamenting.

Helise glanced at the third picture. Yes, here was the banishment of Psyche following her transgression. And yet, it seemed to Helise that something in the vision was awry. What could it be?

The title exclaimed, once more with apparent irony, *Femina varium et mutabile semper*. Her Latin was restricted, but this was a quotation she had heard before. 'Fickle woman is always changeable.'

And indeed, Psyche had altered from carnal curiosity to frenzied terror.

She was depicted rushing down a winding granite stair, her arms flung out, her face ugly and contorted with scream- ing. All the rest of the small canvas conveyed pitchy nothingness – but for one curious whorling hint of motion, seeming to come on behind her, somewhat like a flock of birds –

The door of the tower room shut in a hollow clap.

'You are here with reason?'

Helise darted about, guilty as a robber, almost afraid as one.

'I came to ask of you – ' But no, she had not come to ask.

He stood before the closed door. His doublet and hose were the colour ice, his hair nearly whiter. His face appalled her, it was so fair, so inhuman.

It occurred to her to throw herself on the floor at his feet. She did not do it. Etiquette, which had chained her to a life of slavish unhappiness also prevented such servile extremes.

'Didn't they tell you, Helise, never to meddle with my possessions?'

'I've touched nothing – I was so careful – '

'Why are you here?'

She was too frightened even to cry. She loved him. But who? This god of ice and snow?

'My lord,' she said, in a little voice. Then, 'Oh help me! Everywhere they accuse me – I didn't know what I must do.'

'Who accuses you? What are you talking of?'

'Your mother, the lady – that old woman. I see – I don't please you – but I'd suffer anything – only educate me, my Lord Heros – '

'Crucifixion of Christ,' he said.

The partial blasphemy checked her. She bowed her head and now tears streamed from her eyes. Useless: he would not comfort her.

Presently he moved across the room and going to the table, ran his hands recklessly, as she had not had licence to do, over all the compendium of scales and jars, parchments, mummies, vertebrae. It was even violent, this sweeping, for one of the wired skeletons gave way when his fingers encountered it. At that he took the horror up and threw it across the room. It smashed to powder on a wall.

But when he spoke, his voice had no edge or noise.

'I believe they must have asked you, Helise, if you're with child.'

Something gave way within her.

'Yes, my lord.'

'And naturally, you're not. Poor innocent,' he said, rather as his mother had, lacking all pity. 'You must learn fortitude. Now if I were a sodomite, or impotent, you might divorce me.' (These syllables were like a sentence in a foreign tongue.) 'If you had the will and the power, you could seek an annulment. But do you even comprehend, Helise, how I fail you?'

And she thought of kisses and his hands upon her waist. She burned, but it was ice. She could not say anything.

'I see you nearly do comprehend,' he commented. 'Well, madam. You'll go wanting. I could, but I will not. Understand this. Think me a monk. I'm sworn to chastity. Of a kind.'

'What will become of me?' said Helise. She had made out one word in ten. To inquire of the Infinite was a ritual, like the *peccavi* before a priest, one's mind elsewhere.

Heros had proceeded to the room's hearth (empty), and there he leaned, looking down on the bruises of finished fires.

'There's a dream I have sometimes,' said Heros d'Uscaret, conceivably to the hearth stone. For it was unlikely he would confide in the pathetic wife they had allotted him. 'It began when sin began. I mean, impurity. The body's urge, Adam's rod, that makes him one with the beast, the reptile, the bird, and all the copulating, fornicating mass of lower creation. I remember the first dream. You see, I'd caught sight of a girl, washing herself in a river. The blood rushed to my head, and swelled my loins. I itched with my gluttony. It was manhood, and it was vice. Or, as they tell us, it was the natural order. All day, I could scarcely think of anything but that naiad in the water, laving herself, her round breasts with their eager tips, and the smoky hair in her armpits and under her belly.'

(Helise, arrested, gazed dry-eyed. Her heart raced. But he, he might have been meditating on the digging of a grave.)

'Night fell, and I into the night, and into the dream. Because I was well-schooled by the priests, I had not thought to ease myself. But asleep, the Devil took gentle charge of me. What were my hands doing, there in the dark? How should a sleeper know. And up and up I rode upon that delirious wave that had begun like an itch and mounted to a storm. And there was a pressure in my brain, a green torch behind my eyes – and at the end there came a kind of fit in which I groaned aloud – and then, then, everything unravelled in me. I tell you, my sinews, my bones ran as if molten. And my skull was burst inside out. Where was I then? No longer in the throes of my pleasure. It was a place of mud, and I crouched there. Above were stars that blazed like pain. And beneath me was something that writhed only a very little, and I lowered my face and tore at it, and raw meat was in my mouth and hot salt gushed between my lips and up into my nostrils.'

Heros drew in his breath and let it go.

'I woke in indescribable panic. Sin had changed me. I'd become – I did not know what I had become. But in the dark I found myself with my criminal hands, which had betrayed me to Satan in my sleep. God's benison. I was only myself. In all ways, a boy, a man. In those nights then,' he said, 'I'd have them tie my hands to the posts of the bed before I would sleep. But by my sixteenth year I'd trained myself to wake from the snare before the dream should go very far. Do I disquiet you, Helise? Of course. You should never have come into this room. This is where I look upon my soul. Stupid girl. You see in the picture what happens to the curious.'

Helise, her palm pressed to her mouth, drum-beats shaking her body, turned to remove herself from the chamber.

'You must never come here again,' he said. 'You must forget what I've said to you. Tell no one. Swear it. On your saint.'

In a crumb of a voice, she swore as he required.

He did not, with his emerald eyes, observe her creep away. He was staring once more into the hearth.

All down the stairs, and in the corridors, going south now back across the house of d'Uscaret, to her nuptial bedroom and the room of sitting which were her jail, she imagined him borne upwards on the inexplicable wave, twisting, arched like the Christ on a cross, and his face an agony like the face of Jehanus. And when at last she reached privacy she sank on the wide bed where they had lain side by side, sword by sheath. And she too twisted and turned and was arched on her scaffold, and upon her also came the fit, so her cry rang clear against the ceiling. It was like the call of a bodiless preying thing that flew about there.

She did forget the other element of which he had told her. The meat and wine among the mud and stars: that was gone.

She had only been able to learn one lesson from him.

It had killed her. She had exploded from her own skin, and lay stranded on the pillows. No longer was she an innocent.

She was defiled, she had entered the lists of the wrongdoers. She felt relief. If she was wicked, she need no longer rein herself in. She could admit her wants and where possible indulge them.

When she was in the d'Uscaret chapel now, her eyes on

the prayerbook, she thought, This one never bothered with me. But Satan covets me. *He* will attend.

And then, frightened, she put away the idea.

But in the night, lying alone, recaptured it.

Would Heros ever return to her, to their bed? Surely yes. It was expected that a husband lie now and then with his wife. Such forms he honoured.

But she had learned what had been missed from their lying down. She had learned, by his voice and words, if not his embraces, the communion they might have shared.

Of course it was a fearful thing. Uncanny, astonishing. That escalation, that paroxysm –

She recalled now only that chastity had prevented him. His hands tied that he might not dream of lust.

Helise visualised that she came to him in the dark, and untied the bindings, and his hands fell instead upon her own body.

But although the bed had at last pleasures for her, he did not return to accompany her in them.

Ten nights went by, twelve, twenty.

Having confessed, would he never come back?

She saw him seldom, even at dinner. He was on some business of his father's, Lord d'Uscaret, the peeved man who drank and sweated and kicked at his dogs.

Yet one morning early, going into the Sculpture Garden, Helise beheld Heros walking with his mother slowly up and down.

The garden lay on the north-west side and had high barriers. It was supposed to be a retreat for the women of the house and Lady d'Uscaret would frequently avail herself of its shade in summer at midday. Helise therefore restricted her forays to dewy twilights, dawn or dusk.

She did not like a garden, either. It had none of the quaint simplicity of the courts of la Valle, where figs and vines grew up the walls and flowers lived in pots. The Sculpture Garden was ruled with straight paths, partitioned by yew and box, conifer and ilex, all coerced and sheared to the shapes of balls, cones, squares and other symbols, or if not that, let out into birds with beaks and stretching tails. Where arches crossed the way they were thick with foliage, mathematical hoops of solid green. In the marble water tank was a hairy water-lily, which ate flies, a curiosity: Helise had witnessed a gloating gardener feeding the plant. In the shrubs nested statues. Leaves and boughs strove to swallow the statues up as the lily gulped insects, but this was not allowed. At the end of the garden was a statue of Psyche, so Helise had come to apprehend. She carried a lamp, on her way to discovering her naked, handsome lover.

But one thing was certain, and that was the ease of hiding in such a garden.

A month before, Helise would have slipped away. Now she slipped into the cavern of a prodigious yew, and as he went to and fro with his steel mother, devoured Heros with her eyes.

After the two figures had patrolled in silence for some minutes, the lady spoke.

'You must know, if you take yourself away, I shall have nothing.'

And Helise was amazed to hear the passionless metallic woman say such a thing in her remote voice.

'Mother – I hoped you'd excuse me this.'

'Berating you? You know I won't rail at you, or weep. I shall be quiet. But if you leave this house, my light goes out.'

'The Duke's commission – '

'Is needless. A ploy. For your escape.'

Heros smiled faintly. Helise did not think she had ever seen that before. The lady's hand rested on his sleeve like a long bud of the motionless carnivorous lily. Then it twitched, as if it could not help itself, losing a fly.

'Madam-mother. You must let me go.'

'When you were a child you had these notions. That the City choked you.'

'Don't you prefer me at peace?'

'It's that wife he foisted on you that drives you away. A witless female spawn of la Valle, got by your father for her dowry, because he cannot leave the pots alone.'

'It's true. Marriage doesn't suit me, mother.'

'I've noted your aversion to her. But what is she? Less than one of the bitches. You live your life as you wish, and leave her to hers. She's barren besides. In time, you can slough her for this.'

And then, sick and trembling, Helise saw that he grinned, the beautiful saint's face split like that of some riotous drunk. Not laughter, but this bestial snarl of mirth, quite soundless, behind the woman's head, so she did not even know. And when he answered his voice was composed.

'Oh, let Helise alone. What might her replacement be?'

'But you will remain at d'Uscaret?'

'No, mother. I'll be gone.'

They had halted, there beneath the statue of Psyche with her lamp, for ever frozen in her marble moment, never to reach revelation and despair.

'Heros,' said Lady d'Uscaret, and then, after a second, 'you should have been a priest. If I had had any say – '

'And I mine, mother. It was the only chance for me.'

'That drunkard I wed, that disgrace to our name, that clod. A fool in everything.'

In the umbra of the statue they hung, neither looking at the other, not speaking.

Then she said quickly, 'We must never fear shadows. It strengthens them. What are the nightmares of your childhood? What, you and I to credit a delusion?' But suddenly she seized hold of him. She clung to him, and her flat hardness was like petrification. And he, he bowed his head until it rested on her shoulder. One could not see his face. Yet they were like any mother and son in a scene of awful grief.

And then they drew apart, and this might never have happened.

'In a month,' he said, 'I'll be in another country.'

'As you think fit,' she said. 'Yes. We're in accord.'

When they had vacated the garden, Helise stayed rooted in the tree.

Her stomach heaved as if she were indeed pregnant. But all she had truly discovered was that Heros would soon leave her.

That night, the door of the bedchamber opened. Heros entered. Behind the screen with its running of white dogs and grey hawks, the gentleman undressed his master. Then the gentleman, as ever, discreetly left. Heros approached the bed in his silken robe. And Helise ceased to breathe or think.

'Sad little wife,' said Heros, looking at her not in complacency, or pity, definitely without excitement or intent. 'We did you an ill-turn. I'm sorry for it, Helise. Will you forgive me, and pray for me sometimes?'

'Yes,' she murmured.

'Have they told you? In a few days, I'll be away on the Duke's errands.'

Someone must have told her, superfluously after she had spied.

'Yes, my lord.'

'You'll be glad to see me gone,' he said. 'Believe me, your disappointments weren't my aim.'

Helise let out her breath in a shivering sigh. She did not look at him any more, and he went about the room as usual, dousing the candles, so the dark tide came sweeping from the stones, and followed him to the bed's foot, and there he blew out the last candle, and blackness filled the room and the bed alike. And he and she were alone inside that blackness, like two birds shut inside a cage.

Never before, not even on the first night, had she been so

conscious of him, his proximity, as he joined her in the bed.
The movement of his flesh and limbs against the sheet, the
whisper of his hair over the pillow. She felt a warmth from
him like the radiance of a cool flame.

He did not speak to her again. In a short space, his
respiration assumed the levelness of sleep. Could he really
render himself to oblivion so readily? It was some cantrip he
knew, this knack for slumber.

But she must lie awake and think of him. Of his nearness.
And if he slept, might she not approach him more closely?
Would he wake and chide her?

Helise swam through the sheets and her hands encountered him, as the swimmer in sightless deep ocean
encounters another living thing, with a galvanic shock.

He was naked. Like Cupido, like the god. With her palms
she had contacted his flank, the architecture of ribs under its
suit of skin.

He had not woken, no, he had not. Therefore might she
discover him once again? Or, more crazily, lawlessly, why
not, like Psyche, *look at him*?

No sooner had the fancy taken hold of her than it seemed
she must do it. She could no longer control her need, or
savagery.

She slid from the coverings and sought her way by touch
along the bed, a mile of stuffs and ungiving framework, until
she found the chest, the candle, and the tinder set by.

She struck the spark. She might say she had heard some
noise, or – at long last – that she could not sleep.

But not a murmur of protest issued from the bed. And
when the fire leapt up on the wax, shielding it with her own
body, she glanced about. He had not moved.

Like Psyche, and with all her stealth, Helise stole back
again, along the length of the couch, cupping the candle
flame. The curtains of the bed were drawn back, she had no
necessity, as Psyche had, to lift them away. It was the sheet,
the covers of brocade, these she meant to pull aside.

She must kneel up on the bed. She did so. The candle palpitated and steadied, flickering only with her rapid pulse, as if illumination itself sprang from her heart.

She leaned over him, her left hand now on the coverlet.

His head was turned from her, the blond hair rayed upon the pillow. Bare, the shoulder presented itself to her for the scald of spilled burning matter. She must be wary.

And as she leaned there, her left hand getting its slow grip on the sheet, he stirred.

Helise started away. Instinctual precaution made her thrust the candle aside to the length of her arm. The flame bent, flattened, sputtered – and the room reeled. But he, after all, did not wake. He had merely pressed his face further into the pillow, away from a light unconsciously perceived.

The walls and ceiling settled, the candle-flame resumed its steady trembling. Helise looked down on the sleeping man, and saw the hair had been caught away now from the nape of his neck. A strange shadow emerged at this place, from the roots of the hair, coiling along the spine, to dissolve between his shoulder-blades.

With caution, she brought the candle close again. The shadow dimmed but did not move. Helise leant nearer. She inhaled the clean maleness of his flesh and longed to brush her lips against the flax of hair, and saw the shadow on him was a scar, a curious plating, a trail of tarnished studs – she could not make them out. Like a lizard's scales.

It was a birthmark. (Had not her own maid had a raised discoloured nubbin on her knee, the shape of a star?) Helise put out her hand to finger the mark, the sweet flaw in his beauty – stayed herself, reached again for the edge of the sheet.

She stripped the covers from him deftly, in a leisurely receding wave, inch by inch, her heart hammering in her breast.

Would he wake now? No, he would not. His sorcerous sleep was like a breathing death.

She had never seen a man's nakedness, save in a statue or a painting, there never fully. He had the appearance of both statue and painting as he stretched there in the light amid the shores of darkness, adrift in the bed, his skin more swarthy than the linen, the smooth musculature carved and scarcely troubled with breath. Not stone, perhaps, but some strong ashen wood, tinted faintly to the hues of life, in order to deceive, and equipped with quiescent manhood, something at which the young girl had guessed, dismaying to her more in its first-seen familiarity than by anything alien, the tempter, the serpent of sex.

Careless of the glimmering, burning tallow, Helise bowed over the body of her husband. Her kisses printed themselves along his arm, his side.

But the hot wax did not drop upon him, and her mouth, the helpless small noise she could not now keep herself from making – these did not break in the membrane of his slumber.

He was enchanted. And she dared do no more.

Helise quenched the candle, and removed herself from his vicinity.

He did not rouse even at that.

The chamber seemed distended and tinderous with her solitary sins.

It was because of his aversion to her that he made the opportunity to be gone. He did not want her. If she had been able to cause him desire, how could he have resisted? He would then have remained. He would have been her lover.

But it was a witchcraft on him.

Did a woman then have no skill in such magic? It was the most ancient sorcery, Eve's art, practised at the foot of the apple tree in Eden, that which brought down the race of mankind.

They said, at d'Uscaret, they muttered that Ysanne . . . that Ysanne was clever in women's business.

'Cherish,' had said fat old Ysanne, 'she must overcome her blushes.'

'I'm unsure what is meant. The lady should be plainer,' said Ysanne. Her beady eyes were cunning.

Helise sat in her chair and her humiliation, clenching herself to endure.

'My Lord Heros is tired of me. Now he departs the City. How shall I provide an heir if – if – '

'If he doesn't assist you. Yes. A woman's lot is a rare fix.' Ysanne had changed her tune. Now she and Helise were co-conspirators against the masculine order, conceivably the masculine God.

'They say – '

'And what do they say?'

'That you can make a potion that will – enhance – '

'That will make a girl too good to be left alone. That will swell the male member so it must get busy. I can do that. And several other things.'

'I think – he won't visit me again.'

'Ah, that's tricky. I'll give you a charm. It will call him. If he doesn't arrive directly, then you must find some excuse to bid him. The charm will render him pliable. Then something for his wine, and an unction I'll give you to rub in your skin, very fragrant. Leave it to me,' said Ysanne. 'I've always relished that little chain you wear, with the pearl.'

Helise removed the chain. She held it out to Ysanne.

'No, no. Are you offering that to me? But lady, I serve the house. I'm your slave.' Then seeing the chain flutter, knowing Helise inept, Ysanne quickly added, 'You're too kind, madam. I thank you. It's always safer to seal a bargain. Naturally, this is a secret.' And with the pearl in her bosom off she went, leaving Helise to pace about, between repentance and vaunting, dread and disbelief, praying with untame transgression for Heaven to grant her profane hope.

*

The Bride

She wore the charm, a mouse's sack of herbs, under her shift. Not seeing Heros d'Uscaret by night, morning, afternoon, she sent him word. Through servants, she entreated he would speak to her before his journey. The servants said they had not found him. Further inquiry told her that her husband was dining at the house of this family and that. That her husband was dining at the palace with the Duke. That her husband was in his tower, where they did not venture to bother him except at the summons of his father, or his mother.

Days ebbed. She stitched them into her embroidery, and picked them out again, but still they were lost.

Ysanne's herbal charm did not work. Her other mixtures would be as useless, the unction, the drug for the wine. She would not address herself to Ysanne again.

Then, from a dry husk or two let fall by the voice of Lady d'Uscaret, Helise had made known to her that in three nights, Heros would leave the City. She did not even recall – perhaps they had never mentioned it to her – where he was bound. Whether by ship or overland route. The date of his return had not been coined.

There was a page who sometimes waited on Helise when the household gathered. She supposed he had been designated hers. On the stair she beckoned him.

'Where is my Lord Heros?'

'In House Lyrecourt, across the City.'

'You will follow me now and I will give you a letter for my lord. Then go with it to the door of d'Uscaret and wait for him. Wait all night if you must.'

'He'll be home at midnight,' said the page, perkily privy to the doings of her husband as she was not.

'That's as may be. Only behave as I tell you.'

In the bedchamber by the void hearth, the great chimney-piece with its falcons either side, she wrote: 'Call upon me tonight, my lord, or, such is my misery, I shall kill myself and damn my soul for ever.'

What fashioned these words, succinct and awful, she could not decide. The Devil? It could not be her own desperate mind. She was a fool, but Satan was wise.

But then, would Heros attend to her threat?

It seemed Satan ascertained he would.

She handed the letter to the page, folded in a scarf which she had smeared with Ysanne's unction.

Alone, she anointed her body, rubbing the spicy-smelling oil into her breasts, her thighs, her throat and belly. The friction maddened her. She sprinkled the powder into some wine. She wondered in alarm at all she did. But now, as if a bell had struck the hour, she knew that her prayers were heard in Hell.

She heard too, finally, the midnight Matines tolled from the Sacrifice, and not many minutes after, a dog barked under the wall. It seemed then she felt the reverberation of the shutting of a door.

Time passed, or else time was stilled. And in the midst of the candles' shining, as if in a slab of crystal, Helise waited.

Until the great door of the bedchamber was opened.

On a frame of dark, her pale husband stood looking at her.

'What is it, madam, that you want of me?'

Some feminine slyness had kept her in her gown, her hair bound in its metal caul. The same slyness stayed her on the spot, staring at the floor, her hands clasped under her breast.

'My letter to you,' she said, 'told everything.'

'No, nothing. Are you so desperate?' he said coldly. 'You seem in command of yourself.'

'I die of sadness,' she said. 'But since you don't care for me, I strive to hide the hurt. What do I want? Only courtesy. Not to be the mock of the house. That you should say farewell before you leave me for ever.'

Ah, Satan, her tutor.

Now Heros had closed the door and advanced into the room. Helise did not lift her eyes, although he was before her.

'It isn't to be helped,' he said quietly. 'But since you wish it, I'm here to say farewell. And for this talk of death . . .'

'To kill myself? Why not? What should I live for?'

'You are God's. What worse insult can you offer the Creator than to fling back His present in His face? Do you think He would ever forgive you? Through the endless centuries until Doomsday, He would not.'

He spoke as sternly as any friar. She recalled the conversation between himself and his mother in the garden. To be a priest, his only chance. He was wrong. *She* was his chance. Her love, so strong and vital that it seared, this would set him free.

'You must be my guide,' she whispered.

'Then cancel every idea of self-destruction.'

'I will remember your words. If you were here to guide me – '

'Helise, I can't remain. Sweet girl,' he said, suddenly very tenderly, 'you must guide yourself. Let your own angel instruct you. You're so young – not one iota of blame . . .' And he ceased speaking, and she knew that his concentration was centred wholly on her. Either her vehemence, or Ysanne's ointment, possibly both together, had taken hold of him. She had come to life for Heros, with all that implied.

Saying nothing she turned from him and poured the wine into a glass. She offered it to him, meekly, still her eyes lowered, afraid he would glimpse the fires in them.

'The cup of parting,' said Helise. She employed the phrases of courtly songs, these came with facility, now she needed them, or Satan sent them, for how could she have a vocabulary to manage this?

He accepted the wine slowly. He did not drink, but stood regarding her.

Then, at last, at last, he raised the cup.

She looked, and saw him swallow, once, twice.

'What wine is this?' he said absently. His eyes were fixed on her. At their intensity a wonderful terror submerged her. Never, in any of their dealings, had he studied her in this way. It was the gaze of desire, or so it seemed. He drank again, not taking his eyes from her. And then he frowned, and said, 'There's something in the wine – did you mean to poison me?'

'Oh no!' she cried. Her heart seemed cloven by its hammering.

'But – what is it? What have you done to me?'

'A love potion,' she said. The admission was safe now.

'Then, there's no choice.'

He smiled, grinned with the deadly dead mirth she had witnessed once before, and tilting the glass he drained it, and let it go. It crashed in bits upon the floor.

'Perhaps, Helise,' he said, 'perhaps you haven't been sensible. Come here.' And when she took a step, he took several more to meet her, and caught her between his hands. 'Love potions,' he said. 'Did you think I didn't want you? For every night spent in bed with you, first a draught to make me sleep. So that I shouldn't be tempted. For you're adorable, my white wife. Better than any dream. But perhaps the dreams won't matter now – '

The earth gave way and the room broke off in shards. She clung to him and he kissed her, a kiss of serpents, his tongue in her mouth.

His hands were those of a saviour, supporting, rescuing her in tumult, but also the hands of one who would destroy her, finding purchase on her body, ripping at the laces of her gown –

She had unleashed desire, the carnal entity. His breath burned on her throat. He held her so tightly she herself could not breathe. He bore her backwards and the hard floor was harsh under her uncushioned slimness. His weight pushed her down. A sore sweetness shot through the core of her breasts as he drew on them with his lips. Almost delicious but partly horrible – almost a torment – and then a tickling and probing between her thighs so her instinct was to evade – but he would not allow her now to evade him, and then came a terrible pressure, like that of a thunderbolt trying to cleave her, and she felt she would be burst, but there was only a shrill tearing, like a broken string.

She saw his face as he invaded her. She did not know him. He bore upon her, his skin engorged with lust and his eyes opaque and perhaps unseeing. There seemed no longer any contours to his face. He did not behold her and was unrecognisable. His hair tossed about him, shaggy as the mane of a beast, lank and dark with sweat as if with blood –

The thrusting of his body within hers was a punishment, a horror that was nearly an ecstasy, and far worse for that.

Helise heard herself moaning and pleading in pain. The fire-making action of his loins scorched her. She struggled, and the ghostly ecstasy surged in her again, and she no longer cared what had mounted on her, what killed her there on the ungiving ground. It was not Heros. It was some hideous thing, some creature of the Devil, torturing her in Hell for all her sins –

She heard terrible sounds rising in her throat, and then the spasm hurled her apart. She was screaming. It would never end. In animal fear she let go her clutch upon the excruciating peak, and fell away.

Only then was she revolted, finding herself on the floor, ground into the tiles under the weight of him, a hard mass of flesh that still moved upon her, still thrust mercilessly inside her.

He was lifting himself up, his head thrown back –

On the arch of his throat, the weltered light caught a dull sequin that all at once flashed, and then another, and another –

Helise lay pinned under his racking body. She stared at the altering skin of his throat. It was coming out in tiny jewellery slates, which ran together. His neck was scaled now. It was all a perfect tesselation.

Something scraped along her breast. Her head rolled and she saw a black claw retracting from her behind a thread of blood.

She could not scream. Her screams had been spent. At that instant, the quake of his crisis rocked through her, and it was he that cried out. It was not the cry of a man.

A whirling clotted the air, a fume of candles shaken by a gale.

The sword of flesh unsheathed from her. She was filled only by pain.

Something rose up, many miles high against the ceiling. She did not want to see. Her eyes refused to close.

The shape of a man, but the face, the head . . .

It must be a mask, a visor – it was a bird. A bird's head, formed from a streaming mosaic of scales, but for the blackish carved beak, the thin black worm of the tongue . . . the eyes were green bulbs. There was no intelligence in them, yet there was *being*. They *lived*.

Helise lay on the floor. She had no breath, no reason. Her heart had stopped, her blood was frozen cold. Yet she *saw*.

The thing moved from her, left her. It lurched across the room. It came upon the fireplace and there it squatted, and then suddenly leapt. *It was away up the chimney*. It was gone.

PART THREE

The Jew

I looked to Heaven, and tried to pray;
  But or ever a prayer had gusht,
A wicked whisper came, and made
  My heart as dry as dust.

Coleridge

The Jew had laboured into the night, poring over the antique scrolls, the tablets of wood, the books bound in vellum or horn. Haninuh the Scholar, so they called him. The Jew's House they called his dwelling near the corn market. There was no ghetto in Paradys. No Jewish area even. Those Hebrews who inhabited the City were of the travelled kind, accustomed to a gentile world. Some had committed themselves to the Christian faith, some had given over God entirely in their intellectual venturings. The Jew Haninuh was not precisely of these orders. Then, too, other than the Jewish *mezuzah*, his door was guarded by a Grecian head of Hermes. Called "Scholar", Haninuh was reckoned to be versed in mysteries.

It was not rare with him, to spend the hours of darkness in study. Tonight, however, he had felt restless, and was unable to keep his mind on his reading. The cause of this unease was not personal. Rather it was that kind of nervousness particular to certain animals before a storm.

Haninuh neither sought to quell his discomfort or explain it away.

About two in the morning, he left his books, and went up through his house to a pavilion he had had built on the roof.

69

Here he found, kneeling on a bench before one of the pavilion's open shutters, a small girl-child of no more than eight years, arrayed in an embroidered shift and quantities of curling black hair.

'Now, Ruquel,' said the Jew, 'what are you doing there?'

But Ruquel, who was his daughter by a slave woman long since laid asleep in the earth, only answered, 'What a bad night it is. What shadows there are.'

With these statements Haninuh could not argue. He had been aware for some while that his child seemed to have inherited a sensitivity to occult things; he had already, for her protection, in simple ways begun to prepare and train her.

'Yes, my Ruquel,' he agreed therefore. 'It is a night of some meaning. But perhaps you'll trust me to keep watch in your stead?'

At that the child nodded, and getting down from the bench yawning, kissed her father, and returned to her bed.

Haninuh then took up his vigil in the dark, going slowly from one window to another of the six-sided pavilion. All the shutters hung wide on the close black night, and from this high vantage, at this unlit hour, one saw clearly the brightest stars caustic above Paradys. Below to the north-east wandered the river, coils of which, leadenly glimmering like a dragon, were partly visible between the roofs. Southwards on the heights stood the ghost of the great Church.

What could there be in this dark like so many others, which set the hairs electrically upright along the body?

Haninuh tensed, and leaned slightly forward, his hands upon the uprights of the window. Keen-eyed, he had seen something moving, away along the south-west scallops of the City roofs. This in itself was not bizarre. A cat might be hunting there, or a robber. And yet something in the manner of the movement did not suggest either feline or man.

Haninuh the observer saw again a curious flapping lunge,

like the wing-beat of some huge raptorial bird. Of too large a size –

And whatever went about there in the night was capable, it seemed, of running up stonework, folding itself over housetops, and sliding to the street below like water flowing from a jar.

Haninuh was abruptly very glad he had sent the child to her bed.

Half-unconsciously he murmured, 'From the visions of the night, when deep sleep sinks on men, fear came on me which made my bones to shake, and then a spirit passed before me and the hair of my flesh stood up – '

Haninuh fell silent. The apparition had poured suddenly from view.

There was then a long second of the sort in which, as they said, death might pass over; the space between two breaths.

But then, from the black hollows of the City there tore a frightful wail, a wavering shriek so truly appalling that for a moment the Jew doubted his ears.

The night seemed splintered, and dropped back in pieces. An abysmal quiet staunched the wound of the single cry.

Every nerve a quill, Haninuh poised to see a hundred windows lighted, a hundred people dash out on the streets.

Nothing occurred.

Like a thrown flint, the grisly screech had gone without a trace into the swamp of night.

If any others marked it they did not act.

Only far off a dog or two howled, nearby a rat scuttled. Presently the notes of Laude drifted from a convent by the quays. The stars swung noiseless overhead.

Some drunkard has been throttled in an alley, or some old score settled with a knife. One had witnessed nothing.

The Jew turned from his watch, listening intently now to be sure his own house stayed peaceful. It did. One must be grateful for that. For the rest, it was the world's way.

The vice which tuned and strummed the night had not let

go, but only slackened somewhat. Yet Haninuh was weary. Spared a revelation, he could descend now and sleep, as a soldier slept between his watches.

'Blessed be the Lord at our lying down and blessed be He at our rising. Into thy hand I commend me, my redeemer, O God.'

Next morning, Haninuh awakened with a feeling of oppression. This did not surprise him, nor was it due to lack of sleep. He spoke a prayer of thanksgiving for the new day; in the house above he heard the beaded laughter of his child.

Having some business near the upper markets, Haninuh went in that direction, southwesterly. The route shortly took him into a square with a public fountain. A crowd was gathering here, jostling and exclaiming, and it was impossible to proceed.

'What is the matter?' Haninuh asked of a man in the crowd that he knew, a cobbler by trade.

The cobbler turned to him hotly and said, 'Something happened during the night. A murder in the gate of the tanners' yard. An apprentice found the body not an hour ago.'

'There are frequent murders in the City,' remarked the Jew.

'Just exactly. But not like this.'

'Why, what is its novelty? Murder is murder.'

The cobbler was about to speak when a party of the Duke's soldiers rode into the square and breached the crowd.

Unable to go by, or to get closer, Haninuh waited impassively.

A stillness was settling. The soldiers had grouped at the tanners' gate. Suddenly a woman cried out wildly: 'Oh! Oh sweet Jesus!' And there was a small commotion as if perhaps she had fainted.

Rumour ran like a current back through the crowd. Men

mouthed it in each other's faces. It came to the cobbler and to the Jew. 'The throat and eyes all gone.'

'That's what I heard,' said the cobbler, complacently afraid.

'What does it mean?' said Haninuh.

'Some animal with the madness must have done it,' said the cobbler, 'ripped out the lad's eyes and his throat – and the whole body's in ribbons, and the entrails expressed. He was a poor weaver's assistant coming late from his work.'

'Did nobody hear his cries?'

'No. None at all. A street woman said she thought she heard a yell, between the second and third hour. But one cry can mean anything, even enjoyment, begging your pardon, sir Jew. Then supposedly if it had him by the throat, he couldn't cry again.'

Another man close by, in the apron of the tannery, morosely said, 'They'll want to push the blame on us. We've a feud with the weavers' guild.'

Yet another man said, 'Only a monster could make such injuries, a unicorn, or a tiger.'

Soon the body had been covered and removed. The Duke's soldiers grimly warned the crowd to disperse.

Able to continue on his way, the Jew noticed, under the tanners' gate (the place at which, last night, he had watched the bird-like thing pour down the wall) a black slur on the cobbles, and trampled in it, one pointed, broken shoe.

Violent death, as Haninuh had remarked, was not unusual in the City. Many mornings carried a small cargo of corpses along the river; the alleys of the lower bank were often paved with cold flesh.

Even so, this other death, which thereafter began to be a feature of the nights of Paradys, though frequently un-reported, undiscovered until its unique signs had been obliterated – this death was a different death. It was a rending, *debauched* death. It bore an older mark.

While locks and bars were checked on and enhanced in many a house, the house of the Jew acquired (they said, those that spoke of him) less obvious safeguards. For example, from the street had been noted some bunches of herbs hanging in the narrow lower windows. For the Hermes at the door, it was freshly cleansed, and had been anointed, too, in a pagan way.

The City, where it knew, discussed these matters.

Otherwise Paradys went about its business, as it had always done. As do all cities, like ancient beasts, which, on a strong soiled hide, only idly scratch the little embers of disease.

A month had moved over the calendar and was gone. The Jew walked up into the Scholars' Quarter of the City, along the canals of aged libraries, and by the new university. He went to visit an elderly rabbi, a black-robed old lion, who dwelled near the river.

They sat together in a low-ceilinged room that smelled of books.

'And you tell me you watch every night, Haninuh, from your roof?'

'Every night without fail. Sometimes I detect some disturbance. Never the relevant one. I've seen nothing since the first night. And on that night I do believe I saw a thing, a thing I can barely describe, let alone envisage.'

'Is it not,' inquired the other, 'dangerous for you to watch in this manner? Do you have, I think, a child in the house, a daughter of your handmaid who is dead?'

'My Ruquel is well-protected. I've seen to that above all else, by forms you know I can command.'

'Ah, then. But for yourself?'

'This is strange,' said Haninuh. 'There is that in my blood which recognises this thing as a natural foe. The memory of our forefathers in me contains some glimpse of it, so I reckon now. And have been attempting, from scrolls and parchments I possess, to learn the source.'

'Now I will relate,' said the old rabbi, 'a story of a recent death among the gentiles here. Perhaps you will not have heard of it, for the affair is smothered.'

He then regaled Haninuh with this:

A young girl of good family, closely kept, had let slip to her maid that a gallant lover had begun to court her. He must have seen her on her way to Mass, for this was one of the few times she was allowed from the house. He approached near midnight and somehow climbed up the wall, perhaps by means of the ivy which grew there. Then he attracted her attention by scratching on the shutter. Naturally, the damsel did not go to the window, but, having an imagination, she had already decided on the cause of the nocturnal visitation. Sure enough next morning she found, on opening the shutter, a scrap of paper fixed there with a thorn. Some ill-scrawled words of love (they were later seen by others) and a line of poor poetry, confirmed her in her triumph.

The maid, another silly girl, resolved to help her mistress in the interesting adventure. She spied from a lower window the next night. Sure enough, the ardent lover again climbed to the upper window, and getting no reply, except maybe a stifled giggle, left again a slip of paper with a couplet. The maid for her part was able to attest the suitor was most agile, though rather odd in his mode of ascent. For the rest, she had made out the slim figure of a young man in a cloak who, for his protection, seemed to be wearing some kind of eccentric mask. Later too, in the hideous aftermath when she was called to account, the maid detailed this mask more fully as that of a peculiar bird.

For several nights more, the fun and games went on. Until at last, moved beyond reason, the damsel dared to open the shutters, hoping for a look at her love.

Ghastly shrieks and a noise like blows brought the entire household to her chamber door. Unfortunately it had been bolted from inside.

The girl's two brothers and an uncle put their shoulders to the obstacle, urged on by the most terrible sounds from within. To their shouts, the girl seemed unable to respond. She screamed ceaselessly, as the uncle subsequently averred, like a woman he had once beheld racked for witchcraft. Until abruptly all noises finished.

The door gave in a rush, and the men of the house burst forward into the room.

The window stood wide and empty. Nothing was there, save that there were some black stains and scratches on the wood of the frame. Below and about nothing was visible in the night, except for three of the City watch who had come running at the outcry, yet not in time.

At the chamber's centre lay a fearful sight. The girl had paid dearly for her foolishness.

The wounds were unbelievable, though of the usual type now known, in the subfusc of Paradys, as relating to the rending, debauched death at work there. Her throat was torn out, her eyes . . . there were great incisions in her belly, although interruption had prevented a disembowelling. Quantities of her hair had also been ripped from her head, and were strewn about. Scratches, like those on the wooden window-frame, scored her white throat and breasts. It was presently discovered that, amidst this carnage, an attempt too had been made to violate the girl. But being a virgin, she had proved difficult, and her assailant had not had space to complete the rape.

Now all this in itself was bad enough (though not so much worse than some twenty other like murders current in the City). But the stricken family was next advised by agents of the Duke, that they should not make public either their loss or their quest for vengeance. It was to be given out the girl died of a fever. In return for this favours might be anticipated.

The important houses, though apt to feud with each other, were united in aristocratic respect of Ducal prerogatives. The family, that of Lyrecourt, did as bidden.

It was further believed that the girl's body was burnt rather than buried, a priest counselling cremation. The corpse, which seemed to have been attacked by a giant bird, was accordingly rendered into ashes.

'It is thought, too,' added the old man, 'that the corpses of all females assaulted and slain by the creature, have also been incinerated.'

Haninuh sat brooding. At length he replied:

'There is more to be feared of it than death only?'

'So it seems.' The rabbi laid his hands upon a little book of black leather, with a lock of damascine steel. 'Myself, I have been searching for this demon. Though I lack the courage to look for it in the dark, there are other darknesses. After some trouble, I found this volume, which is a fragment of a larger work sometimes called *The Book of the Night*.' And saying this, he pushed the book across the table to Haninuh.

On the black cover was embossed in silver the Solomonic Seal, and in one corner, a *menorah*, also in silver.

'Here is the key, Haninuh. Take it away with you, and read the passage I have marked. But no other. I can trust you in that.'

Haninuh assured the rabbi that he might.

Soon they parted, and with the black book fastened into his sleeve, Haninuh went back across the City to his house.

It was in a small chamber set off from his cubicle of study that Haninuh unlocked the book. The door was shut on him. There was no window, and the space was illumined by a single candle of honey-wax.

When he had cleaved the book, with much care, at the place where a flat wand of bone divided it, a faint light seemed exuded from the vellum, and then to suspend itself upon the page.

The text was on the left side Hebraic, and on the right in Latin. Haninuh read, comparing each text with the other as he did so.

'There was a man in the fort at Par Dis, at about the time the seven-hilled city of the Romans, and all their empire, fell. He was a soldier, a centurion, having charge of a cohort, and from Roman lands. And at his death, he left his arms and honours in the temple of Mars here, marked for him *Re Va*, which temple being excavated, has preserved them in the City with many others.

'Now this soldier, after some misfortune, had recourse to an amulet said to have been fashioned in Khem.' ('Aegyptus' said the Latin.) 'However, the amulet had its origin in the country of the Assyrians, possibly at the City Calah, in the days before David was King in Israel.

'Now the Assyrians worshipped all manner of idols, and were beset by all the races of the demons. The amulet took its power from just such a being, an *utuk*. Its shape was graven on the jewel of the amulet, and was that of a man, but having claws upon the feet and fingers, and the head and beak of a bird of prey.

'At first the Roman found that the amulet was helpful to him. But then, it seemed to draw away his strength, while the demon began to haunt him. At last he assayed riddance of the article, but through this very means was enslaved by it for ever. Thereafter his line was polluted by the demon, which was wont to manifest itself among his descendants here in Paradys. Its method was this, that it was carried in the semen of the male and the blood of the female, in the way of some poisons or diseases. And as with disease, a proportion would prove to have a natural resistance to the effects of the pest. Therefore, generations might pass without any sign, though all were tainted, until one would be born who was vulnerable, in whom the *utuk* could get a hold. For the *utuk* was given its life through metamorphosis and shape-changing. The woman who was susceptible would birth a son or daughter infected by this evil, most often the former. That man was then, once grown, capable both of transmuting into the form of the *utuk*, and, through his seed, causing other women to conceive a similar mis-creation. In this case, tainted kin, or not, all women were impressible. It has been recorded, there are further permutations to this generative transfer at the injection of seed, but no document had been discovered regarding them.

'The *utuk* is in itself a terrible thing, a ravening thing, which craves human life in its form, and more sensually in a robbery of blood and flesh. It is an Eater, a Devourer.

'Though magical safeguards are of protective use, the *utuk* itself, while possessed of a human host, is impervious. For the carrier may be killed through any normal means, at which the demon makes its escape by whatever route is to hand, into another host, for an example in his infection by the spilled blood. Where no transference is likely, that aspect of the demon may be considered extinct, providing the body of the carrier is burned and the ashes laid. However, though every individual manifestation of the demon be destroyed, in its poisonous disease-like form, it remains inherent in that kindred it has afflicted. Who are by name the *Vuscarii*.

'For the amulet itself, it is lost. The hue of it is said to have changed, as do particular jewels when heated, or exposed to wear. This tint, the shade of the jewel as it was or has become, is believed to offer warning through a colour of the eyes of those contaminated.'

Haninuh, having gained the end of the text, replaced the bone marker, shut up the book, and locked it.

As he did this, the candle flickered wildly and would have gone out, but the Jew spoke at it a Word, and the Word stayed the candle flame, which burned up straight and still once more.

It was night, and there was no moon.

Haninuh paused at the threshold of his daughter's apartment. She had been washed in a little bath of lettuce enamel, and, her prayers said, got into her bed with her wooden doll and her striped cat. There all three were, staring at him clear-eyed, doll, cat and child.

'And are you ready for sleep, Ruquel?'

'Yes, father,' she answered, and put her doll into the sheets with its tow head on the pillow, while the cat purred and kneaded the covers.

'Have the bad dreams stopped, little girl?'

'Oh yes, since you put the water dishes out to catch them.'

'You must tell me if you dream anything bad again.'

Ruquel smiled. 'I say to her,' she nodded at the cat, 'we're safe. You won't let anything hurt us. Though she was frightened when we had the dream. But not now.'

When he had kissed all three goodnight, as was obligatory, wood lips, soft lips, fur cheek, Haninuh climbed up the house to the roof pavilion.

Blackness hung over Paradys, the book of night open randomly at the darkest page.

As usual Haninuh performed three rituals, and uttered some prayers which, upon white deserts and obsidian mountains, had long ago invoked the benign forces of fierce angels.

In just such centuries, the Jews had kept vigil against the hordes of Assyria. They had fought with them sword-to-sword under skies of flying arrows. The wolf-like Assyrians, whose cities were lilies of a river bank, had riven Israel. And Israel had brought down upon them the bolts of the one true terrible limitless God. Until the people angered Him, and He turned from them, and then the Assyrians leapt at the throat of Israel . . . it was all to do again.

From those times Haninuh's soul remembered the demon. The *utuk*.

Night lay motionless on Paradys, yet it moved towards the east. Haninuh heard the bells ring for the offices of Christendom, the hymn of drunks from an alley, smelled the corn

market, and flowers on the house vine, saw, heard, smelled
nothing from the ordinary.

About two hours after Laude had sung from the convent
near the quays, deep weariness overcame the Jew. A longing
for sleep weighed on him. Soon it would be dawn. Though
hidden senses told him grim events had gone on somewhere,
he had been vouchsafed no clue.

He rose from the bench and made his way towards the
pavilion's door. His hand was on the latch when he heard
a muffled scraping and rustling from nearby, on the wall.

Sleep dropped from him like a mantle. A chord of sparks
shot across his body. Something was coming through the
vine, up the side of the house.

Haninuh turned to confront the six unshuttered windows
of the pavilion, his back to the closed door. He did not have
long to wait.

A black lump of darkness came sliding over the roof's
edge and slewed across two windows, enlarging itself into
the third.

Haninuh, back to the door, the third window before him,
whispered, 'I believe with perfect faith that the Creator,
blessed be He, is the maker of all things created . . . I believe
with perfect faith that all the words of the prophets are true
. . . I believe that the Creator . . . knows every deed of the
children of men, gives heed to all their acts – for my salvation I hope, O Lord! I hope, O Lord, for my salvation! O
Lord, for my salvation I hope!'

Blackness, and from the black a sort of twisting into form,
like a man's, but the hands were talons and clacked against
the pavilion wall – and out of the black leaned something.
It was the head of a bird composed of the green sequins of
scales, and a beak black with dried blood, and two eyes like
emerald.

There was no intelligence in these eyes – and yet they
were, they *lived*, they *knew*.

'In the presence of my enemies,' said Haninuh, 'You are

with me. Even in the valley of the Shadow, You are there.'

The beak of the *utuk* cracked apart, and a snake tongue whipped outward and in again. The eyes were smoky now, as if drowsy. It came and pressed on the open window – and started off again. It had struck the invisible lines of power that barred every aperture of the Jew's house. And it did not like them; perhaps they stung.

At that instant the Jew woke into movement. Casting before him a cabbalistic incantation that smashed the etheric lattice of the window, and seemed to carry him with it, out of the pavilion he sprang, snatching up as he hurtled through a sword of honed steel from the bench.

In that moment, in his blaze of fear and rage, the magus Haninuh touched terror with his body, came knee to knee with the unearthly, deathly thing, and with a moan of dread raised the sword, on which the names of angels, the script of most arcane talismans, were scored –

But the horror shuffled off from him, like the nightmare. It evaded the stroke, flounced on a flightless wing-beat away, and over the rooftop, smearing and roiling itself in, getting like an ape down the wall. The fragile vine was ripped now, and fell with it into the street. There in the pure black the beast of night disappeared.

Haninuh stood and trembled.

He had been too slow, yet too strong for it – or else, by flight it mocked him. For it was drawn to him as he had sensed it might be. A traditional foe. Doubly in danger now. Worse, he had let it escape to continue its mayhem. For this hour he had planned, but he was found wanting.

The Jew bowed his head before his own failure, consenting, bitter.

PART FOUR

The Scapegoat

Remember me – Oh! Pass not thou my grave
  Without one thought whose relics there recline:
The only pang my bosom dare not brave
  Must be to find forgetfulness in thine.

Byron

For thirty-nine days she was their prisoner. On the fortieth she was their victim. It was her punishment. She knew that she was guilty. She had looked for no kindness, and her first actions were prompted by the habit of human commerce, not fantasies of pity.

The truth had come to her gradually, as if she returned to consciousness: nothing had happened to alert the house.

Even her screams had been those of pleasure, and doubtless, if anyone had overheard them, they were correctly interpreted.

The metamorphosis occurred in silence.

It had been visible only to herself.

At the recollection – the *full* absorption of what had taken place in front of her – Helise wrested herself to her feet and swayed there in her ripped gown, her hair raining round her shoulders. She felt herself dirtied, bloody. But the only wound, of course, was one which would be acceptable, despite the fact that it was out of date.

Nevertheless, her helpless need was to seek others, to raise her voice to a new pitch, and tell what she had been the witness of. That this was not believable did not cross her mind. She had watched. She had no choice *but* to believe.

83

Some while it took her to recall how a door was to be opened. That achieved, she went out into the corridors of d'Uscaret, almost wandering, and coming to a lighted spot, she did raise her voice, and began to scream. Once begun, this expression was not easy to leave off.

People came. She did not know who they were. Shadows jostled on torchlight and the eyes of candles blinked at her.

What she screamed, if there were words, Helise did not afterwards know.

Presently someone struck her in the face. She fell down, and looking up from the stones, beheld Lord d'Uscaret. One of his rings had cut her eyebrow. She felt the numb hurt of it and putting up her finger, caught a bud of wetness.

She was now quiet and they dragged her to a room. Here the kindred gathered and glared on her. The servants were shut out.

Lord d'Uscaret paced about. His wife sat in a chair and gnawed her lip. For a long while they did not ask. At length, this question: What did Helise mean by her noise?

Helise said, with the clarity of an honest child, 'When he lay on me, his face and head became the head of a bird.'

As Helise said this, Lady d'Uscaret let out a single sharp cry, as if she had driven an awl into her hand. Then she rose and left the chamber. Her face was awful, as though its bones had collapsed and no blood was anywhere under her skin. One of the men followed to support her.

D'Uscaret came back to loom above Helise, and he was sweating as he did at his evening drinking.

'Who told you, you witch, to say such a thing?'

Helise was confused and did not answer.

Then d'Uscaret slapped her again, and though now the rings did not cut her face, she darted away, and fell once more, and crouching on the floor she said, 'He never would, my husband Heros. But tonight I made him, and he lay on me, and when the thing happened to him which happens, he altered. His flesh broke out in metal spangles, and I saw he he had a bird's face, and the beak, and a demon's eyes, like a hawk's eyes, but green. It ran away up the chimney.'

D'Uscaret turned from her. 'Go search the bedchamber.'

Pale as their lady, two of the men went out. The few left behind looked half-mad. D'Uscaret sweated. Not one of them had declared these events must be impossible.

Helise saw that her statement seemed obtuse, which was mostly due to a lack of carnal vocabulary. Feeling no reticence, she tried to put this right. 'I mean,' she said, 'that when he was being a husband to me, when the fit comes, then he was changed.' Suddenly a wild lament swept down on her. Tears gushed. She sprawled on the floor.

Shortly after this, everyone went out, and locked her into the room.

Helise wept until all awareness was wrung from her body. Perhaps she slept then.

She wakened to torchlight. A steward of the house, and a woman who waited on Lady d'Uscaret, pulled Helise up-right.

'You will make no sound,' said the waiting-woman.

They took her through the mansion, along passages, up stairs, rather as she had taken herself earlier, searching for the secret apartment of her beloved.

Finally there was another room, with sparse furnishings, a window of lactescent glass. A ghostly servant had arrived before them, and was putting out a ewer and cup, a covered basket. One candle burned.

The servant, the woman, the torch-bearing steward, drew off from Helise, until she was alone in the middle of the gloom.

She said, stupidly, and for no real reason, 'What am I to do here?'

'Stay, at my lady's will,' rapped the woman.

Then they went, and closed the door, and locked it on her as the other door had been locked.

Helise crept to the neglected, ill-prepared bed. She felt

nothing, no fear, and no alarm, no longer the agony of sorrow. She slept again, and only realised, reviving to sickly awareness at the entry of light through the vitreous window, that she had been imprisoned for her crime.

They brought her food and water and a small amount of wine, her tiring table and embroidery, fresh linen. The room was cold, was summer waning? Although she sometimes asked the servant, they sent no logs for her fireplace, and only allowed her one candle at a time.

There were no writing materials, and if there had been any, who would have agreed to be her messenger? Besides, to whom should she apply? Her family of la Valle had loved her only in as much as she had been wanted by d'Uscaret. Now d'Uscaret hated her.

I prayed to the Devil. He granted my desire and now collects his fee.

She slept a great deal, and dreamed of Heros. Nearly always he was breaking in to rescue her. But overcome with lust, they fell at once to coupling on the floor or bed. In the midst of this she would try to push him away, shrieking. Also she would dream she lay down and the pillow slowly changed into a staring, decaying eagle's head. And once, that her aunt's pet bird flew out of its cage and went for her eyes.

She would wake in fear, or crying.

They gave her no news. One morning, in desperation, she had muttered to the dull unkindly servant who brought the food, 'What do they say of Lord Heros?'

The servant sent her a glance.

'Nothing, madam. He's away on his journey for the Duke.'

Helise was bemused. Later she began to see that d'Uscaret had used the proposed excursion Heros had intended, on Ducal business, as the excuse for his vanishment. He had merely set out a day or so in advance. The City, and half d'Uscaret's own household, were handed this tale, and would accept it. Probably it was put about that he hurried to escape the difficult young wife, who now turned hysterical at her lord's absence, hence her confinement to a remoter region of the manse. Had even the Duke himself been deceived?

But meanwhile – where was it that Heros had gone to, or that thing had gone to he had become? Thinking of that all her nerve deserted her. She had a vision which seemed almost palpable. She imagined the creature on the roofs of the City, at upper windows, perhaps availing itself of chimneys. It flickered in and out of her inner sight. What it did she could not be sure. But they were deeds of darkness, hunger – and in the end it would hide itself. She did not know where.

However, she had one other dream, and only once. She saw the thing (*her husband*) seated in his chamber in the very house, at that table under the round window and the trip-tych of Psyche. Among the paraphernalia of former studies he had paper, pen and ink, and was writing . . . she saw what he – it – wrote. Even in the dream . . . incongruous. For they were rhymes of love. She had not wanted to approach, had been afraid, but the creature did not see her, for in the dream she was incorporeal. Besides, its head lolled, the eyes were dull, and the tongue ran from its beak. The hands wrote busily, alertly, the claws scratching the paper. Some human facet of Heros, some memory from his man's brain, plainly supplied the task, at which the bird's head moronically attended.

Close by on the desk, among the apparatuses of silver and glass, the balances and skeletons, lay some strands of hair, caked with blood at one end. There were also several teeth in a pewter dish, fresh and white but for the old blood on them.

After this dream, Helise did not cry out or sob. She got up as if tranced and went to her tiring table, where the mirror was, and stared in at her own young, shrunken face.

She had never before realised that her eyes were of this

shade. Definitely, if looked upon closely, there was a greenish cast to them.

On the thirty-eighth day of her captivity, Helise was visited by her second mother, Lady d'Uscaret.

The woman entered the room and had the door shut behind her. She wore the black and viridian of the house like mourning. All her hair was covered. Her collapse, which seemed to have maintained itself, had not softened or fleshed out any part of her.

'You may stay in your bed,' she told Helise. 'What else are you good for? I came to look at you. To see this insect which destroyed my son.'

Helise lay with the covers up to her chin, and endured the looking-at.

'Merciless Heaven,' said Lady d'Uscaret. 'Is it a fact, you made the old fool Ysanne give you aphrodisiacs of Alexandria? Don't bother to speak. She was beaten, and confessed. A meddling wretch. But I am to blame. I judged the tales were lies, or advised myself they were. Who could live otherwise? Sometimes, one would say I was green-eyed. I should have guessed from that. My mirror reassured me. But the mirror was old and cloudy . . . And my son, that beautiful boy from such a loveless match – there are such eyes in other houses, other lands. Why attend to a legend, a story to frighten children with at the hearth in winter?'

She spoke in a composed, indifferent way.

'And you. I reckoned *you* harmless. He had his night, so I thought. There is proof, I thought. He took pleasure with her, and no uncommon thing occurred. He had always feared it. Unspoken. I would never listen. Until we walked in the garden, not long ago. "I must be away," he said to me. Then I knew. He'd left you untouched, was virgin still. The curse was in our blood. He dared not.'

D'Uscaret's Lady looked on with her eyes not green, nor black.

'But you forced him to it.'

Helise was nailed on her pillow. She could not move or reply.

'Make no mistake,' said her second mother, 'I'll have you killed. Expect it. Some bane in your drink, a cushion pressed to your face. Or a strong man will come and hang you.'

In her coffin of a bed, Helise could not even feel terror.

Lady d'Uscaret opened the door and went out of it, and it was locked again.

That, and its after-taste, were the thirty-eighth day.

On the thirty-ninth day, women filled the chamber.

They pulled her from the bed, washed her and dressed her, combed out her hair. There was a spurious air of the preparation for the bridal. No one said anything to her, nonetheless. They did not even address her as "lady" or "madam".

When the women had gone, without explanation, Helise sipped the watery wine of her confinement, wondering if it had been doctored. She seemed to have a burning sensation in her throat, but then it passed.

In the afternoon, men of the house entered, without preamble or apology. The steward said to her, 'You must get up, and come with us.'

'Where?' she said listlessly.

'That you'll learn.'

Where she was not an article of barter, or a sexual pawn, she had never been treated as an adult, only ever as a baby, save some of the cruelty might have been restrained in a baby's case.

She went with them, and they took her away along the corridors and stairs, and she noticed the rotted tapestries, the lost chests mice had chewed. She did not pay much attention. She had no say in the world to be interested in it.

Finally she did know where they carried her. She began to scent their fear, and then her heart stumbled and in their grip she almost sank down, but they hauled her on, up the twisting stair into the Bird Tower. The door was in front of her with its ring and falcon's mask. A hand flung it wide, and straight off the step she was lifted, into that chamber, that cell of the scholar, which had belonged to Héros d'Uscaret.

At the hour they gave her no reasons. She was nothing to them, useful only for her femaleness and expendability. It was later that, by small sproutings of gossip, by a letter or two uncovered from forgotten cabinets, such things, that the brain of Helise evolved and ordered a theory of events.

Her dream of him, as he wrote the uncouth verses, had verity. She was spiritually linked to him, she, the author of his damnation. In the moment of union, two becoming one . . .

No sooner did she enter the room with d'Uscaret's men, that thirty-ninth day, than she glimpsed the strands of hair, the teeth in the dish, ink spilled on paper, on the floor. He had left other marks in that room, once so esoteric and cleanly. (The painting on the triptych had at last been overturned. Perhaps this was some vestige of human anger, or only the upsetting of flight.)

The Duke had sustained d'Uscaret, and one other great house had reluctantly held its vengeful arm. But there had been atrocities in the City. Not only a daughter of Lyrecourt was won to a couch of blood, not only the rich and mighty howled for an end. The Duke had said, it seemed, he would leave d'Uscaret to its own affairs, whatever their nature, providing d'Uscaret would see to them.

It did not always come to shelter by day in the Tower of the Birds. No, only seven or eight times did they detect it had entered there, going over the roof and in at that round window inaccessible to any other. It would possess scattered eyries. The vaults of chapels, wild land about the old City wall; it had been seen climbing the turret of a ruined church, by a man who took it for a monkey – but some, hearing the rumour, knew otherwise. Elsewhere, near the markets, two fornicators were scared in a corn-bin by a beast they swore was a giant beaked lizard that had on man's clothing.

Yet the human memory, some urge, brought it now and then to d'Uscaret, and most often by night.

It could be slain. No legend had ever prohibited that. How, was less sure. And they were afraid, sickened, loathing. Something must be put between them and the actuality.

A drinker and feeder, it had another proclivity. The horrid reports had made this obvious.

Lord d'Uscaret stood before the narrow monk's bed, and pointed to Helise, his daughter by marriage.

'Put her there. Tie her. The cord round her waist, with enough slack. Let her go about the room if she wants. He'll smell her the sooner and come in.'

Like a bitch-dog then, they leashed her by a rope-girdle and a long tether. Nowhere in the room was anything that she might employ to hack herself free. She would not even have thought of it. The inevitability of their plan, of which she was so strategic a part, of which she had at that time scant grasp, gave her over for their use.

They did not assure her men would be waiting, with drawn swords, with javelins and clubs, below in the lobby under the twisting stair. They were not, anyway, there for her protection.

A watch would be kept on adjacent heights of the building. She would not even need to scream. She was the bait inside the trap, the distraction, the scapegoat for all their sins.

Like Psyche, sacrificed on the mountain to save the rest.

'He may not come tonight, or tomorrow,' said d'Uscaret. 'We may have to wait.'

A priest in black said solemnly, 'We must go down and pray.'

They were glad to leave the chamber, with its strange tang, faint, like that of a hawk's mews. Glad to leave the scapegoat. The priest, who she had not seen till he spoke, did not offer her word or look.

She roamed a while on her leash, up and down. She could not quite get far enough to right the triptych, or to finger the elements on the table.

For her sustenance had been left white bread in a napkin, fish and mushrooms, cheese and grapes, milk and wine, and sweets.

She ate with appetite. She was not frightened. She sang softly to herself, for company, as she had done in childhood.

When the dark began to come, she spread herself on the low bed. He had slept here, her husband.

She lay and thought of him, and suddenly her body was alive with desire. She longed to feel his weight lowering itself upon her, his caressing ravishments, the thrust of him against her womb.

She remembered a tale at least as antique as the dooms of d'Uscaret, of the monster transformed to human beauty through love's kiss.

Was it a miracle she might accomplish, she who had sent him into Hell, to bring him forth again into the light?

She lay in the blackness, and her body moved with the rhythms of fire. She slept, and dreamed his weight crushed her, his strength pierced her. She was opened out, stretched to her limits, her brain shattered in stars.

But nothing but dark and dawn entered the chamber, the thirty-ninth night, the fortieth day.

The window was a bowl of jade, translucent twilight.

Helise gazed at it, surprised to have slept so long.

On the floor the panier and plate were empty. The food

had not been replenished. A mouthful of wine was left. Shadows curtained the room, and silence had spun her web there. Helise shifted again on the bed, and sang a phrase of song, to hear the web quiver, then regather on the frame of the dusk.

The rope had begun to chafe her ribs where it had ridden up over her gown.

She lay and watched the window ebbing from green jade to marzipan grey. She might sleep again. Sleeping was benign. She had dreamed of loveliness, though she could not recall it now.

Drifting, she heard a mild scrape-scrape at the window as if far away. A leaf or branch, unsettled by some evening wind. Or a bird against the panes. She was not inclined to look, to try to make it out.

She drifted on, borne by a smooth river, the room a dark forest that rustled gently, and blew upon her an open breath of sky, until she bumped against the wharf of awareness, and her eyelids raised themselves.

Where is this place? Not a forest, but a chamber, its one green eye now black. The aroma of a mews was stronger.

Then she heard. A crisping of garments, a step on the floor. She heard, there in the darkness, unseen, a *breathing*.

'Is it you, my lord?' she called softly, 'my Lord Heros?'

And the breathing was arrested, began again, and drew nearer.

Somewhere deep-buried by forty days in a wilderness, Helise d'Uscaret knew that she should, at this second, be whimpering or shrieking, weak with horror, tearing at her fetters, crying to God. But all she felt was a slight curiosity, a glimmering want, to see again what she had shaped him to. And even in that, lust moved, lust murmured like a tide within her. She was under a spell. She was the Devil's dupe. She was damned as he was.

'Is it you, my lord?' she said again, and held out her arms.

The reek of a preying bird was thicker, musky, and there was too another darker flavour, like the scum of a marsh. The stink did not repel Helise. It intrigued her. Even the butcher's whiff of blood did not offend.

'Heros,' she said.

She felt more than saw a blacker blackness between her and the window, beside the bed. Then the eyes, catching some flake of light from the sky, flashed, and turned on her their soulless motes. The eyes of Satan, pendant there in nothingness, this they might have been. But she was not afraid.

Then, from the bedfoot, the heat of a body came crawling up on her, the weight of the body covered her, and two hands slipped across her, her breast and throat, and there the talons scratched her, but it was glancing and inadvertent.

In the dark, she put up her own hands and touched the roughness of the scales, and the emerald eyes floated, watching her, seeing her as she could not see, in the dark.

He had not harmed her before. She had not been told what had been done, out in the City. Her images of those things were nebulous.

Something swung across her face. It was the wicked beak, but she did not realise. Instead the questing, ugly, (invisible) tongue extruded, and sipped at the skin of her neck, strayed across her breastbone. Sinuous and serpentine, it described the mound of one breast.

Lying on her, the monster from the myth made love to her in the blind dark, as in the blind dark the Unseen had made love to Psyche.

Helise, who should have doubted, should have lit the lamp of her ordinary virtue and cancelled love with howls and screams, clung to darkness, which had the arms, the muscled back, the thin pelvis of a man, and which filled her with the organ of a man.

She must not cry aloud, even in ecstasy –

Just at that moment, as she twined him with her limbs, on

the crazy threshold of abandonment – just then, Psyche after all kindled her lamp.

Beneath his body, some black filaments of clothes, her eyes dazzled – she was conscious the door had been pushed wide, and the torch glare streamed into the chamber.

Her silence, as maybe her screaming would have done, had betrayed them.

Helise attempted to speak. To rouse her lover, to ward off the spurl of fires and men, the glint of weapons that came pouring down on them.

But the lover of Helise, he knew. He knew, and did not leave her. As his loins thrust on, frantically, against her and within, the head of the monstrous bird was turned, to look sidelong into the crowd of assassins.

A look. It stopped them. The men fell back. The weapons were folding over like blades of grass before a scythe.

A sound came out of it, the thing that rode upon her, and turning again, it buried its fearful head among the pillows.

Helise clutched at the shuddering muscles, cloth, silk, flesh, scales – the crowd in the room had no meaning. Enormous beats began to echo through the core of her, and in the insanity of delight, she beheld a woman like a long opaque shadow, push by the wilted kindred, the strengthless swords. In the carnivorous hands of Lady d'Uscaret was a soldier's spear. Her eyes were all the face she had. Her eyes were no longer black, but blazing green.

The shock of the javelin, rammed into the body of her son by this woman, who thrust with death as he himself thrust with the weapon of life, rocked both lovers like the quake itself. And Helise felt the point of the spear, tearing through his heart, prick out to graze her breast.

She gaped her mouth to scream after all. And on a backcloth of lights and shadows, where the woman seemed to topple away (like a flat figure in a church window), there was a spurt of blood, a falling, a throe, of generation and of terminus.

Helise, between all the many gates of Hell, was thrown into the Hell of ecstasy.

She shrieked and writhed and a spear seemed to enter her also.

In this state she was, flailing and lurching on the bed like a broken snake, until they dragged the dead thing out of her and off her, on to the floor.

Then, only then, the delirium guttered and extinguished. And she was left behind.

She lay, covered in his blood, soaked by that, by tears and sweat, and the waiting-woman of the mother of Heros leaned over her and said, 'Drink this.'

Helise drank. She had no choice, for they held her.

Long after, she became convinced that all the people had gone away.

When she sat up, it was so. The chamber was black and shut, as earlier.

When she stumbled from the bed and pulled herself on hands and knees across the floor, she encountered a bloody spear, but nothing else.

They had taken their dead away. They had left her here with their poison in her to die in her turn.

Already she could taste death, and in her arms and legs it stole like cool water. There was no pain.

Sitting by the hearth, she attempted to perform a contrition. Would God hear? God had never heard her.

Eventually she was in the fireplace. Still, she was not afraid. Her body was cold, but for her heart, and then her heart was cold too.

She felt it cease, she felt herself die. It seemed irrelevant, pointless.

What happened was this:

The Lady of d'Uscaret went to her own chamber, and there she hanged herself. She was buried in state in a family mausoleum near the Temple-Church. It was explained she perished of sadness, learning her son had been killed by robbers on his journey. His body had been lost in foreign lands.

For the bride of Heros, who took her life at news of his death, there could be no holy ground. But out of compassion they made her a bed in the walled garden.

Not much after that, a feud sprang up between the houses of d'Uscaret and Lyrecourt. Its foundation was obscure, some insult or obtainment. Despite the stern jurisdiction of the Duke, the flower of d'Uscaret's young men were soon mown down, and the lord himself was slaughtered like a pig on his way from Mass. At least, his soul went well-prepared to Heaven.

Inside a year, all the candles of d'Uscaret were put out. A few of the kindred, obscure relatives, old women and men, lingered in the mansion with their elderly servants.

A decade, and d'Uscaret had become little better than a lodging house.

Though there were yet some who, passing it at dead of night on the street, would cross themselves under its walls, not knowing why.

PART FIVE

The Widow

Be a god and hold me
With a charm!
Be a man and fold me
With thine arm!
Browning

As if from the tomb, sleepily, he rose up from her narrative.
(Which might be apposite enough.) She had anyway bewitched him. He had seen what she said, in vivid pictures,
masterful paintings come to life.

Raoulin stirred, and stretched himself, as he would not
have done so freely in the presence of a lady. He took care
not to look at her directly, but into the pallid glow of the fire,
which had either been fed while he sat entranced, or which
magically never went out.

'But Demoiselle Helise,' said Raoulin, sportive with the
supernatural for there seemed nothing else to be, 'if you
died, here you are, and you haven't yet given me the
alchemical formula for that. Besides – am I to take you for
twenty-five or twenty-six years? Not more than eighteen,
surely?'

'Time for me has made a stop,' she said. Her liquid
voice thrilled him. The voice of a sorceress. One could not
be blamed for anything under the same roof as a witch.

At his own thought Raoulin struggled briefly. He reached
back after the dead prostitute, the anguish that had brought
him here. But a balm had been salved over them. They did
not hurt any more.

'Shall I,' she said, 'conclude my story at once?'

Then he had to look at her. Into her eyes like emerald. He nodded. She said, 'That part's swiftly told. The poison my husband's mother had administered was insufficient. I did not die, but lay inert, flexible and wholesome, and with a slight breathing that some doctor ascertained. They did not have the heart for more murder, to finish off the bitch's work. The feud was out with Lyrecourt, the Duke's frowns glowering. And there was Heros to be seen to. His corpse had rotted in one night, with a fearful stink, all bits, human and avian. So they made my tomb, and named it for me, and laid the box of his bones there under a proud drape. For me, I was hidden again in this room, and sometimes tended. After many months, it seems I began to revive. I recall nothing of that period, not for three or four years, rather as the infant does not. Then I became myself, and remembered what I had been and what they had done to me. I was content to be hidden, and to hide. I heard tidings of their various deaths from servants. One evening I was told how Lord d'Uscaret, my second father, had been bled on Satan's Way, under the Temple-Church. I laughed and had to pretend it was weeping, because I was still nervous of my jailors.' Helise put up her hand and rested it on her delicate chin. 'You see, Sieur Raoulin, it had driven me mad. You can't anticipate from me any fine feelings. I cackle at corpses. I burst into tears at the newborn baby's cry.'

Raoulin shivered. It was not her words, only some latent truth inherent in them for all mankind.

'When most of d'Uscaret had gone, I began to win out of my prison. I was let go about. I caused no trouble with my walking of the corridors, my occasional peeking into cupboards. I learned a little, but did not take up arms. Like the old ones dying here, I was only and all acceptance. Now they think of me as a part of the masonry. I do as I wish. The two servants feed me and serve me when necessary. Of course, I'm spoken of as one deceased. They recall that much, it must never be admitted, my resurrection.'

When she said this, Raoulin was not moved to horror or distress for her. She seemed only reciting the part of a character in a drama, and not even very well. Her passions were dead even if her heart went on beating. But she startled him next.

Her voice had an avidity when she said, 'Yet, I've waited.'

Raoulin found himself, bewitched or not, on guard.

'For what, lady?'

'Why,' she said, 'I think, for you.'

'For me? I can't assist you – or, if you've some petition I could go to the courts with it – my father has some influence, but not in the City – and do you think – the tale, being or seeming, improbable – '

'No, m'sieur. Be at ease. I want nothing like that.'

Raoulin was ashamed of his reluctance, yet now, as reality came back to him, uncomfortable as blood returning to a numbed foot, he began to yearn to be done with this. In the eldritch room he had formerly deemed coy and feminine, the miasma of her history shimmered. What hour was it? Surely Laude had struck –

'I might have roamed the City, but that wasn't in me to do. My early training was as a daughter of a noble house. You'll understand, Sieur Raoulin, only aged men have recently entered d'Uscaret.'

Raoulin found himself staring at her again, into the jewel eyes.

'Women also may burn,' she said. 'I've been chaste as the nun for all these years of my widowhood. The last violation, the monstrous intrusion – never, since then.'

While she had recounted those things, though they seemed enacted before him, they had not aroused. But now, abruptly, with an extreme pressure, lust possessed him. He got to his feet, not meaning to, and clumsily jarred the table where the wine cup stood – and he thought of the wine, Ysanne's drugs of Alexandria. And through the murk two ideas struck clear, like rocks in a flood. That despite everything, she was a woman of a line older than the City, higher than he could ascend with safety, and, of course, that though his flesh throbbed for her, he did not want to lie down with her, even in a falsehood, the resurrected girl who had pleasured a demon.

But there in the firelight of the sorcerous hearth, Helise d'Uscaret was combing her blonde hair with her fingers, she was shaking her tresses so they flew about her like white foam from the sea. She was putting up her hands to the nape of her neck, the lacing of the gown. 'Come here,' she said, 'and help me.'

And he discovered he was there behind her, eagerly fumbling at the undoing of her dress. And as it slipped from her shoulders, she drew his hands around her body, over the shift, to her breasts and belly. The fire shone through the linen as through the strands of her hair. The scent of her drenched his lungs, his mind.

'There's a pact between us,' she said. 'This must be.'

'Amen,' he muttered, and pulled her around to have her mouth.

Indeed, could you credit her story? Yes, she was insane a little. The prologue to an enticement, all that rigmarole, with the old hag of the kitchen an accomplice.

Somewhere in his brain, like a bell distantly tolling, some tocsin of unease kept on. But he forgot it as he brought her by the carved posts of the bed, and she threw off the shift and lay down before him like a nymph of pearl.

She gave a low laugh when he entered her. It deterred him half a second. Then she had flung up against him, and he could do nothing but begin with her that dance of death called procreation, the invention of the fiends.

Her cries came like those of one under torture. He lifted himself, and saw her, her face contorted with ravening agony or joy, her whole body pulsing as if rivers broke beneath her bones, as if she must dissolve. One look and he too was set off, like cannon by tinder. He leaned on her groaning and an exquisite needle seemed to pierce through the centre of his loins, into his spine, so he also shook and struggled to be impaled or to get release.

And at the height of it, somehow he began to see her again, to see what clasped him and gave him this, and even in the instants of orgasm, some quarter of his brain started to rip at him, to tear him back into his senses. That quarter howled. Then sight and thought smote him together like blows.

Raoulin shouted out – not in pleasure, not now. He tried to spring backwards, and fell heavily against a post of the bed. There, he lay. He lay looking at Helise. At what Helise had become. *Became.*

The fever-image had been correct. For she was, it was a fact, dissolving. Her flesh was slopping off, the skeins of muscles showing, melting in their turn, pouring over the bones like heated wax. And the bones themselves were sere. As they came poking up through the deliquescent body, it was revealed they were old bones, meant to be naked a decade at least.

She – no longer *she* – was a sludge, silt or mud, upon the sheet. And the bones rattled slightly, settling in their improper bed. About the skull, the brittle flax of hair, going every minute more to mould and dust. And in the death's-head, all stained with the passage of sudden decay, two green gelatines were fixed, the eyes of what she had become, of what had allowed her corpse to live, *in waiting*, all these hungry years.

THE PURPLE BOOK

FROM THE AMETHYST

PART ONE

The Roman

Easy is the descent to Hell
Black Dis gates stand open night and day.
Virgil

The Roman stood under the wall of the Insula Juna, listening to his wife crying in the room above.

The apartment was on the first floor of the block; in the street, it was but too easy to hear her lament, through the hot noisy afternoon air. Perhaps she cried more loudly only to be heard by him, her heartless husband. Once she detected the sound of his horse's hoofs she might leave off.

Better get on then. Better allow her the chance.

He beckoned briskly, and the boy came from under the platanus tree with his cavalry mare. Vusca tipped him a silver denarius, that was the sort of times they were. The boy ran off, and the soldier mounted up and started the mare moving.

Lavinia's threnody unravelled along the walls.

As he rode through the shadier back lanes around the temple of Venus, and out on to the broad East–West Road, he thought of Lavinia as she had been, the girl he married. He first saw her in an orchard, just west of the town. He had gone out for the hunting, and come back chastened by unsuccess. The sun was low behind him, the dusty road fringed with dark trees that glowed after the day as if they kept the heat. On a curve of land that looked down to the cemetery and the town's west gate, was a villa one always passed going this way. It was a modest building, by now in need of some repair. Like all Par Dis, it had seen kinder days. Then, over a low wall, appeared the orchard, and by the plum trees in the mellowed light, this girl. Her skin was luminous, succulent. Her dark hair, drawn back into a simple knot, had mostly come unbound. He fancied her at once, and hoped she was some nicely-dressed slave. But although she looked admiringly at him in his leather tunic, the casual-wear of the Fort, and as recognisable as full parade armour and cloak of Tyrian purple, she did not answer his polite greeting, and next ran away. She was fourteen. She was not a slave, either, as he presently managed also to find out. When he started to find excuses to go back along that road, when he started to gossip with the stray servants, or beg a drink of milk at the villa farm, when he saw her very often and realised that she herself found excuses to be there at such times as a passing officer might happen by, then he learned she was the ward of the house.

She was a Christian, as well. That he liked even less. He was himself a Mithrian, and had the mark between his brows. He sensibly worshipped Mars, too, the Warrior, for his profession, and gave seasonal respects to Jupiter the Father. The odd mysteries of Jusa Christos put him off, what he knew of them. It sounded like Greek Dionysos, without enough wine.

He began to frequent the house, though, and became friendly with her uncle, the guardian. He was allowed to talk to her, then, and here and there they sneaked off and furtively fondled. He saw he would only get what he wanted by marrying her and that there were advantages in that – for though rough, the villa had some money in it. Then he wondered if they would insist he become a Christian. But that was not their formula. Apparently he might do as he wished, providing he let her practise her own religion.

He saw later, once he had wedded and bedded Lavinia, had had her, and installed her in married quarters at the Insula Juna, that the whole point of this understanding was that she should then attempt to convert him, day and night long. Those were the first arguments.

He did not mind it too much. He was a Centurian Velitis. His bed was in the Fort.

She next withheld her favours, to punish him for not wanting some priest to push him in the river, half drown him, tell him all his sins were washed out, and now he must love his enemies.

'You forget, Vinia,' he said. 'I'm a soldier. *My* enemies I kill.'

'The armies of the Emperor are upheld by Christian legionaries,' she said promptly. Obviously someone had told her what to say. It was probably true, and if it was, accounted maybe for the great running cracks that were dismantling the Empire. There were certainly no legions left by now in this hole of Par Dis where, like a fool, seven years before their meeting, he had got himself sent. Someone had said the best means to promotion were the difficult and savage postings. And Par Dis, with its town of baths and basilica and circus, was not even so bad. It had originated from some silver mines, hence the name (for Pluto-Dis, god of the Underworld and its riches). But the silver ran out after a few decades. The Empire had been ever-stretching in those days, however, and saw no harm in making a frontier station on the site. There were already roads, a fort, a native settlement. The walls and town were added. The river was useful in the trading way, and sometimes provided fine oysters.

The oysters were all gone now, like the silver and the two legions. Only men of the Auxilia, native companies under Roman officers, held the line in this flung forth province.

He had had his promotion. He had reached centurion, with a command of skirmish cavalry. There he stuck.

It was a curious idea: when he was travelling the miles here from Rome, to begin all this, Lavinia had been seven years old. For seven more she grew up, lying in ambush for him on the west road, coming out with the plums at the fatal moment.

When she would not have him, he went with the amiable whores at the *She-Wolf*. One evening the drunk uncle stormed to the Fort, and made a fool of himself (and of Vusca) over it. How could he (Vusca) be such a barbarian, wasting his strength on these women, neglecting his wife, when all she longed for was to bear him a son.

This turned out to be a fact. Lavinia had now decided to pine not only for a Christian husband, but for a baby.

She went and lived in the villa a while. When she returned to the married quarters, they were reconciled. She had become thin, scrawny with dissatisfaction, or sadness. Her mouth turned down and there were two cut lines either side of it. He did his best. But he did not seem able to please her now, even in bed. They tried for her baby in grim sweaty grindings.

One day she was pregnant. He, less interested than she, made the correct offerings. He supposed she merely praised her ghastly slaves' god, who refused presents with typical petulance.

It was a bad winter. There were wolves at the gates. Uncle went wolf-hunting and was mauled. He died a week later and when Lavinia heard she miscarried in the fourth month.

After this, she did not conceive again. They eventually left off the dutiful grindings. He went back to his whores and she went off to her Christ. When Lavinia met her husband, she would cry. She greeted him in tears as if after an absence of months. Then they would talk, attempting to be rational. But soon her niggling would commence, her whining. She could not seem to control it, like foul breath. At last he shouted, or he was cold, or he mocked her. Finally all he was able to do was leave her, and hear her crying again, from the street below. He tried to enact this repetitive scene as seldom as he might. He had only come here today because she sent him a wild message. He had got the impression she was ill.

But she only said she had had some dream. Her god had told her something or other. And that Vusca and she must return to full relations.

She was using her god now to drag in the erring spouse. If he had been a Christian, it might have worked. He could not think why she wanted him. As lovers they had nothing, and as two people, nothing.

She stood there, fragilely brittle and dry as a dead leaf somehow preserved. One tap, and she would be in pieces. His annoyance would not resist that. They might separate, he said. She was not, after all, by blood more than somewhat Roman, and had relatives in the north. Surely she would prefer to go to them. And perhaps, if there were a divorce, she might (he grimaced, who would want to?) remarry, more happily.

To a Christian, divorce was unacceptable.

She had not married a Christian, he reminded her.

He, she said, had undergone a Christian marriage.

To please her, he said.

He had loved her then, she said.

He apologised, which was cruel.

She cried. On his cue, he left her.

The East–West Road ran straight through the town, straight through the forum, with its market, law-courts, temples, straight on to the East Gate and the Fort. The plan of the town was still pure, whatever else crumbled, whatever slums accrued, the two highways unswerving as ruled lines, the original buildings symmetrical. Above the town, to the south, west, east and north, were the endless ups and downs of the hills that held the river valley. The route east, the view of the hills, even the bustle of the forum – when going in *this* direction – cheered Vusca up. The sight of the Fort itself, though it was the cradle of his disappointments (his life had had little besides), had a look of home which the Insula Juna never did.

Vusca was a man who preferred to be among men. He distrusted women, did not understand them. The life of the legions suited him, with its fellowship of the march, camp or barracks, the orderly routines marked out by trumpets. Though he had yearned in his youth for more active service, now even that had stopped its gnawing. The practice skirmishes of his corps of Velites ably substituted. He realised it was a kind of make-believe. They all indulged in it: the code – that they were ready to repel the hordes, and could do so; the symbol – of Rome astride the world for ever. Rome was not going to last. She was tearing her own heart out. For the hordes, they were those same smiling tribesmen who had their hutment the other side of the river, who bartered with the Fort and in the market, sent stray daughters to train in the brothel, or crossed the water entirely to take up Roman ways, like Lavinia's grandfather. One knew the horde was still there, of course, behind the friendly obligement, the tunic or *dalmatic*. It could turn into a snarl, that smile. And then what? The other bet was, Rome would pull the Auxilia in as she had pulled in her legions already, leaving the frontiers bare, letting go. Then you must decide on marching home to the Mother you could scarcely remember. Or deserting.

No, Vusca did not delude himself. He simply, along with the other centurions, and doubtless the Pilum Commander, lived in the moment.

One thing, if the Auxilia was recalled, he could go to Rome and leave Lavinia here.

He was thinking of this in the forum, and its wryness amused him, when he saw a woman coming down the steps of the Temple of the Father and Mother.

There was nothing in that, everyone but the Christians – and sometimes even some of those – went to make offerings to Jupiter or Juna Anga. But she was not dressed like a Roman. Her garments looked more Eastern, and her face was covered by a wisp of veiling. There was an element in her walk, provocative, liberated, that suggested the hetaera rather than the she-wolf. A Greek prostitute's freedom. No doubt she was a whore, for she had that other look, too.

Something about her aroused him, even as he sat on the horse fresh from Lavinia's howling. Desire did not come so readily now. He wondered what it was about this one that stirred it. He was not even close enough to catch her perfume.

Behind her trotted a slave, hurrying with a parasol like a huge pansy-flower to shade her mistress. They went away towards the Julian Baths.

Vusca rode on towards the Fort.

'There's a new woman. She's set up house behind the Julian Baths. The chief Lupa's roaring. Reckons this one will put her girls out of business.'

Dianus laughed, and the dark sunlight of evening glinted on his eyes and on the silver of his service bracelets.

'Ah?' said Vusca cautiously.

'An Eastern bit, or so they say. I've not been there. Yet. Her name's some foreign thing, Lilu, Lillit – so they call her Lililla.'

'If she's an Easterner, she'll be a Christian.'

'The Christians can't be whores, their thighs are done up,' said Dianus. 'This one worships properly.'

'I maybe saw her,' said Vusca.

'You maybe did. Come and see her again. Or do you want to go back to your wife?'

It was dusk, and up on the roof-walk of the Light Tower the men were igniting the brazier. As they walked away from the Fort, the flame fountained behind them, Dis Light, for a guide to the river traffic, for a warning to any dreamer on the hills: *Rome is here, and Rome is still awake.*

The evening was thundery, close and hot. Fireflies blinked in the bushes of a garden. Dianus swaggered. He was not a man Vusca had ever liked, but yet, like a brother he had grown up with, he was accustomed to him, prepared to be loyal.

A trumpet sounded *gates* from the Fort rampart, now several streets behind. The whole town took its timing from there, rising with the sun at *cockcrow*, securing its door at *gates*. All but the wine-shops and eating houses which were blooming out on the dark like the fireflies.

They did not go by way of the forum, but cut around to the south. Beyond the Julian Baths was a maze of side lanes. Here Dianus located a modest house that had once belonged to a minor official of the basilica. A baker's that took up the front was closed, but over the house door hung a shining lamp of expensive Aegyptian alabaster.

Dianus rapped on the door.

After a pause, a male voice spoke up. 'Who's there?'

'I,' said Dianus flirtatiously, 'and a friend.'

'Which house are you seeking?' obtusely demanded the porter through the door.

'The house of Lililla.'

'This is that house. Is my mistress known to you?'

'Soon she will be,' said Dianus. And losing patience, battered on the door.

A growl answered from within, not human but canine. Dianus stepped off.

'By the Victory! I think there's a real wolf in there.'

'Take yourself away,' advised the porter, over the growling. 'My mistress receives no one without invitation. There are men and dogs here.'

'So I can tell,' bawled Dianus. 'Keep her then, your bloody mistress. But she'd have done better not to fall out with the Fort.' He waited, listening to see if this did any good. It did not. With a volley of oaths Dianus strode off. Vusca kept pace. He was more tickled than anything. Whores came three to the denarius, but this one, as he had suspected, traded by the Greek mode.

He considered the woman Lililla slowly. This was not the hot haste of his passages along the west hill after Lavinia.

Lililla was available for an honest price. The dealings of harlotry, if not of women, he grasped.

Eight mornings later, when the drills, and a store inspection, were over, Retullus Vusca went up to the forum and searched among the stalls and shops. He ended up in the cave of discreet Barbarus (a blond hill tribesman, now more civilised-Latinised than half the town, and capable of speaking Greek more honed than the Pilum Commander's, though this latter was not difficult). Here was found a suitable article. A painted vase of Aegyptian *nard* – a most generous, but not effusive, down-payment. It was dispatched to the house of Lililla by one of Barbarus' own sons. The papyrus read: 'This from your admirer Centurion Velitis Re. Vusca. If he calls upon you this evening, may he hope not to be refused?'

A smaller papyrus reached him before sunset at the Fort.

It answered: 'Lord, I touch your gift to my heart. Come.'

This time the door was opened and the porter bowed.

Lamplight, and a pleasant foreign smell of other oils and incenses filled the lobby. The atrium was the old way – it was an old house – partly unroofed, with a tank of water, but it had been made attractive with Greek lamps and the paint redone on the walls. At the shadow's edge stood a man with two wolfhounds on leash, just visible, a tactful reminder.

In the central room Rome ceased, and Par Dis too. It became an Eastern pavilion. Silk ropes, draperies, images of ivory. On glowing charcoal burned sticks of something that the Pharaohs might have favoured.

Vusca found himself suddenly excited and nervous, like some boy.

He planted himself firmly, and as the slave went out, looked round and saw the woman, Lililla.

She reclined on a couch, in a fringed robe that gleamed like water even as she breathed. Her lips were nacred and her eyes all kohl. She got up without hurry, and came towards Vusca. When she reached him, she kneeled down with the liquid boneless movement of a snake. She brushed his foot with her fingers and got up again, and looked into his face.

'The centurion honours me,' she said. Her voice was low.

He discovered he had no words. He had meant to play her game with her, all courtesy and fakes. But everything about her was sex. Though she was not to be tumbled like the she-wolves, heated and quick, every line of her said *Take me*.

He would have to leave it all to her.

Perhaps that was the idea.

She conducted him to the couch, and gave him a wine bowl of silver. Lovers performed acts thereon that, when he caught glimpses, startled him. The wine was black and spicy. Something in it?

Soon, she made him lie back upon the couch. She undid his clothes with damning competence. She began to do things to his body, with her hands, with a fan of feathers she took up, with smooth strigils of enamel. He need do nothing. She worked on him like a complacently smiling physician. She removed her own garment only when he had showed himself ready, as if to reward him. She was small, with round breasts, round heavy hips, an indented waist, strong thighs. Her feet and ankles, like her hands and wrists, her face, were delicately shaped. She was fleshy but firm, like a satiny fruit. Her lips were the same. When she absorbed his penis into her mouth he was half alarmed. She seemed to have no teeth. When she drew on him, he almost could not check himself. He held back with some trouble, wanting to possess her. She seemed to read this from his eyes, let him go and mounted him, and took him in again at the second mouth, the mouth he wanted most.

She performed all the labour, she also controlled him with a wicked, subservient mastery, not permitting him to ejaculate at first, reining him by a strange pressure at the base of the column. When his seed did spurt, it came in a convulsion. He had seldom if ever known a climax so intense. He found, astonished when she removed herself from him, that she had also penetrated him.

She went away briefly, while he lay there, and returned freshly robed, carrying the wine-cup, which she offered on her knees.

Unlike the other whores, she had made no pretence of her own pleasure. Neither had she shown a whore's aversion, any impatience or indifference. She had been created for his use. It was as natural as that.

When he had drunk the wine and sat up, she said, 'It grieves me that my lord must leave me so soon. But I too have some tiresome business that must be completed this evening. I shall number the days, until my lord's return.'

Vusca was better able to take up the game, now. He said, 'I'd meant to buy you a present, Lililla, but found nothing worthy of you. If I left this purse, perhaps you may know of some small thing that might divert you a moment?' He reached among his clothes and handed her the purse, open just enough she could see he had been generous again.

'My lord's kindness will enhance any gift a thousand times,' said she.

Vusca was aware his kindness would go straight into the coffer.

When he left he was untired, for she had done all the work, and the extreme ejaculation seemed to have robbed him of nothing. He felt fit and jaunty, and congratulated himself on having found her. Though she was rather costly, he could afford a luxury now and then. He had no others.

He began to visit Lililla quite regularly every third or fourth week. He did not know who her other clients were (certainly not Dianus). They were reticent, and so was he.

He and she never talked, beyond short beginning and concluding euphemisms. She wanted no conversation. She wanted, though never appeared interested in, only money. On several occasions, if he was willing, they did things he had never before heard of, let alone experienced. These things were never strenuous on his part, and she seemed a creature with wax for bones. She always welcomed him smiling, and with an obeisance. Her face was not loving, or liking, bored or sly. It simply *was*, without pretence. She was perfect.

Until, near the summer's end, Retullus Vusca went to the house of Lililla and everything altered.

That was a rainy twilight, with a lilac tinge to the hills and sky. Even the stones and plaster, the tiled roofs, had a mauve, wet, lizardskin sheen.

He knocked, the porter admitted him. In the lobby he smelled that the aroma of the place was wrong. The gums burning were swarthier, more cloying. In the tank of the atrium the rain plopped. They walked around under the covered area, and the man with the dogs was absent.

The central room was in a mist, a sort of damson gloaming like the streets outside.

The slave shut the doors. Vusca saw where the smoke came from. A large skull, perhaps of a bear, sat on one of the inlaid tables, and resins were fuming out of it.

She was on the far side, dim through the smitch.

He said harshly, 'By the Bull, can't you get rid of that thing.'

Then she stood up, and he saw, with a peculiar clutch somewhere in his loins, that she was clad like some kind of priestess. One breast was bare, and her body bound in a tight garment crossed diagonally by white fringes. On her head was a wig of mulberry black, in ringlets with silver discs on them. Her arms were gripped by bangles of slick black lacquer.

Was this some new sexual gambit? He did not care for it if it was.

'Lililla – ' he said.

She said, 'Lord, I have had omens. When this happens, I am not my own. Come here, you must attend.'

He was disgusted. Very nearly frightened. And there was the same slithering in his veins he had felt at the initiation to the Rites of Mithras, when he was only seventeen.

He had a veneration for the gods. After a minute, he went to her, and when she told him to sit, did so, gazing at her through the choking smut from the skull.

Presently she started to croon, to sway like a serpent. He thought of the sybils, inhaling volcanic vapours, prophesying, reading riddles. He did not want this to occur. He did not want any of this. He decided, sourly, if she was prone to this, he would not come here again. It was a shame, but he might have known there would be a flaw.

She stopped crooning and swaying.

The smoke was thick in his nostrils, his mouth seemed coated by it. Through the pillar she abruptly said, 'You have never had any luck, centurion. Should you relish some?'

It was so unlike her way of speaking to him. Even the timbre of her voice was higher and slightly shrill.

He said, 'Don't be impertinent. I don't come to you for this. I respect your gods, but my business is my own.'

'I spoke of luck. Is it not true? All you hanker for you miss. Your days with the legions left you here. Your promotion you did not have. Your wife is barren and not fair. If you go to hunt, you kill nothing. If you dice, you take the Dog.'

'You've been asking questions about me,' he said. He added, measured, 'You bitch, don't forget who I am. Rome is the power here. Insult me, you insult Rome.'

'Rome is far off. You are not Rome. You are a man who stinks of his disappointments. All your days are marked with blots. I say again, should you wish to change it?'

He swore at her. (How different from the rest, this ultimate dialogue they had managed!) His mind said clearly, She speaks only the fact. Whether she has gossiped or is wise, she does not lie. I am who she says. Change it? Yes, I could wish that.

Just then the smoke in the bear's skull flattened in a most striking way, as if some vortex sucked it down.

He could see her directly now, before him. Her face was white, her eyes like pebbles. This did not seem to be Lililla. Something had taken possession of her for sure. Some god. Some thing.

'If,' she said, or the god said, through her, 'you accept what is offered to you, reach into the skull. Remove what is there.'

Vusca found it hard to look away from her. He made himself do so, looked at the fuming skull instead. The smoke was almost laid now. It clotted in the cavities of the skull-eyes, foamed at the rim. Still he could not see past it, into the hollow case.

'If you accept,' the woman repeated, 'reach in. Remove what is there. It will be yours.'

Suddenly, like a boy who is dared, he could not put it off. He thrust his hand, or as much of it as he could, into the baked smoke. And felt something on the hot crusts of the gums. He brought it out. It was warm, glassy, black with the smoke as his hand now was. He brought forward a piece of his damp cloak and rubbed, and the mauve rain-light of sky and hills was shining there on his palm.

It was a small oblong of amethyst, an amulet, presumably, for it was incised with the figure of some protective deity – Vusca scrutinised this, uncertain of its form.

Lililla said, 'You have taken it now.'

'Yes, I've taken it. But it's precious, this stone.'

'You gave me gifts, lord,' she said. 'I render to you a gift.' It was the other Lililla, the perfect harlot. He looked, and saw she had returned, and was kneeling there beyond the table, with blood behind her skin and sight in her eyes. Even the wig and the costume looked only garish now. It was the smiling face of mere being. 'The amulet is from Aegyptus,' she said, 'the wine-stone.'

'That is Thot, then,' he said, 'cut into the surface.'

The image had a man's body, a bird's head. Thot, the Mercurius of the Aegyptians, was bird-headed.

Lililla did not reply. She went away as Vusca sat there staring at the jewel, turning it in his hand. That she should give him something of high price seemed odd. Perhaps her gods truly had made her.

The stone was no longer hot. It had assumed the temperature of his palm. It seemed made of his own flesh, only harder, and more smooth.

The woman came back with her hair loose and her silks, carrying the lewd silver cup.

Vusca stood.

'No,' he said.

She stood in her turn, looking at him. She continued only to smile and only to be.

'I've left the money on the table,' he said. 'This jewel's worth more.' He said, to test her, 'Do you want it back after all?' And made a movement, as if to hand it to her.

At that she gave ground. She stepped off three or four steps, quickly. The smile stayed. She shook her head, smiling.

'No, lord. My omens told me. Yours.'

'I never heard of a woman of your sort,' he said, 'giving the client a payment.'

If she had fallen on him with all her most cunning caresses and amazing tricks, he could not have had her, not then. She had spoilt all that.

As for the jewel, probably it was some stained crystal. If it would be lucky – well, he was due a little luck.

It was dry dark outside. Dogs were baying a rising moon.

He walked down to the north wall, had a drink with the sentry captain at the river gate. Below, the water spread to catch the moonlight, and on the other side were the thatched huts of the native Par Disans.

Rome was far away. Perhaps this very hour, she was

burning again, broken. They would be the last to know.

A day later Dianus, meeting him by the quartermaster's cubicle, informed Retullus Vusca the lily whore had decamped. She and all her trappings had vanished away in a night. The house was empty. Hopefuls, who went in to rummage, found nothing worthwhile. Someone said the Lupa at the *She-Wolf* had paid her off.

On his hard bed in the officers' block, Vusca asleep was walking through a long narrow corridor whose ceiling almost brushed his head. The walls were whitewashed, but took no light until the way opened into a courtyard. In the dream, Vusca glanced about ironically, responding as he tended to, to foreign things. The walls of the court, like the corridor, were whitewashed and painted over, with lions and chariots. The other end of the court gave on a flight of white steps going down to dark water under a tight drum-skin of heat-drained sky. Palms grew against the steps, and in the water pale cupped lilies and purple-coloured lotuses.

An overblown altar stood in the court near the water-steps and a man was making an offering there. He was naked but for a kilt of dressed skins. His body glimmered like metal from sweat or from oil; his hair and beard were curled. The incense steamed on the altar, it had an overpowering smell, almost kitcheny, like something cooked or fried, like offal, and like musky sweet things, too.

The altar was carved with creatures that had male bodies, wings, the heads of lions, rams, birds.

Sun hammered out the river. The man's flesh and hair shone. The streamer of incense rose.

Nothing else happened.

When Vusca woke, the trumpets were sounding the third watch. Here, it was night. Known, every angle and shadow of the cell, its two chests, the lamp, the chair which had once been uncle's at the villa, the weapons on the wall and the bearskin he had bought from Barbarus one bitter winter. Beyond the door, left open, the mathematical Roman yard, with a ray of light playing down from the torch on the Praetorium wall.

Vusca heard the trumpets out. Then turning on his side, returned into sleep, and did not dream again.

On the evening of the Wall Walk, the Commander elected to lead the squadron. Formerly, there had been a manned sentry-post for every half mile of town wall. In the lax climate that now prevailed, only ten posts were kept up, besides the south, west and river gates.

Every month, at the Calends Moon, one of the ranking centurions took the Walk, a tour of the entire wall, which lasted upwards of four hours. The Fort mason was supposed to accompany the presiding centurion, but normally contented himself with a question or two the following day. Otherwise, the Walker was supported by his adjutant and a block of ten of his men who would have been happier in the Fort. For the Pilum Commander, he seldom if ever took the Walk, as he seldom bothered now with the Night Inspection, delegating this also to his Centurion Secundo or whatever officer was most handy.

Vusca had overseen Nights more times than he could count, and the Wall Walk nearly as often. He learned that he was not to escape on this occasion either. The Old Man wanted both the mason and Vusca for escort, with ten Velites (who as usual would fret and feel insulted, since for the Walk even the cavalry went on foot. In the old days a skirmisher division would never had been put on such a duty. But then).

Dianus spoke scathingly of the Commander. 'What's stirred him up? Afraid the Emperor's watching from afar?'

Vusca shrugged. He despised the Pilum Commander, who liked wine too much and spoke Greek like a pimp and Latin like the fishmongers' descendant he was. Long ago, Vusca

had partly hated the man. Yet even in those days Vusca
served him impeccably. A soldier must honour the command, if not the dross which might fill it. One did not tar-
nish one's own vow because of a fool, a stroke of rotten luck.
Nor did one, like Dianus, yap about his faults. It was part
of the great pretence that every commander be sufficient.

They started out just after *gates*. There was still a flush of
light in the west, mauvish (like that other night). It was
autumn weather now, and the remainder of the sky swagged
low with cloud. They would probably get a wetting before
the Walk was done, which made it stranger still their
comfort-loving Pilum had decided on it.

He strutted ahead, like a barrel on legs, in that dress
armour of his with the inlay of silver, iron cap plumed with
its white coxcomb, and the Tyrian cloak swaggering, full of
wind. He was jovial too, and cracked the odd joke with the
mason. Centurion Velitis Vusca kept the proper number of
paces to the rear, his Velites marching with a dull clink and
clash behind him. At the manned posts, the Commander
received the salute with theatrical earnestness. He spoke to
the handful of sentries, encouraging them in the wind and
light spat of rain that was beginning, as if enormous enemy
battalions lay below on the garnering night. A couple of
times, he called Vusca up. The second time it was: 'That
man to be disciplined. Sloppy. Probably drunk.' Vusca
accepted the criticism on the man's behalf. His name was
Quintus. He had bad teeth and sometimes dosed himself
with poppy. It was irregular but understandable. And was
the drug more distracting than constant pain? The Commander, of course, knew nothing of any of this.

They got down to the river gate inside the first hour, the
tour had gone briskly thus far.

The Pilum paused for a drink with the sentry captain,
complained about Quintus, had another cup against the
dank evening.

Out on the wall again, behind the Commander's cock-sure, rolling advance, Vusca heard one of his men mutter, 'He thinks he's going to his Triumph.'

Vusca, for once, saw fit to be deaf.

In the second hour, marching over against the north-west hills, the rain began to come from Jupiter's slingers. It lashed the right cheek, whistled into the right ear, blinkered the right eye. They tramped on, shimmering iron men with seaweed cloaks. That clown, with his damned plumes, carved through the rain, wine-insured against the weather.

They reached the west gate. This time Vusca was invited to join the drinking. He touched the flagon with his lips.

The core of the storm came when they were on the western stretch, with the rain striking their backs.

For some reason, Vusca thought of a minor engagement in hill country, all of thirteen years ago. The downpour had started in the hour before battle, slanting on the ranks, and up had gone the shields, to make a tortoise against the rain. He was reminded of the sound of it now, a barrage like nails, hitting those hundred or so crossed lightnings, torches, the Medusa faces and snake hair washed and slapped. They had fought in the rain too, skidding and sinking in the mud, while the sky flickered with levin-bolts. They won, that went without saying. When the tempest lessened, the barbarians lay everywhere, while the rain gently cleansed their wounds. His infantry shield remained with him to this day. It had a hole through one of the Medusa eyes where someone had almost finished his unpromising career.

A white crack suddenly wrecked the sky. Everything leapt out stark and dead, a place with no dimensions, colours or shadows. Lightning was here, too.

Then came the boom and shock of heavenly ballistas.

One of the Velites shook himself as he marched, with a rattle. Water down the neck.

Not alone in that, thought Vusca. He watched the Commander rolling on ahead, impervious it seemed. Even the mason had dropped back. The next manned sentry-post was visible, ten minutes away, and below, the town, wild on this side, bothies and brothels, though along the slope the ruined circus stood up like a raised scar.

Vusca turned his head and saw, across the streaming night, the dim glows of the easterly town, the spark of Dis Light on the Light Tower. He felt together a dismal sense of futility and a raw pride. He had come to care for it, this outcast place. Perhaps, when Rome was only a pile of rubble, Par Dis in exile might survive.

More rain went down his neck like a cold lesson. *Remember you are mortal.*

So much for the whore's amulet. Even now, like a dolt, he had it in a pouch round his neck. It surely failed to keep him dry.

And then the world blew up.

There was just a dot of white and then a drench like fire. As he flew, turning, falling, he thought, quite distinctly, he had known something like it before, but he did not know where or when – an earthquake maybe, or a nightmare.

He landed hard, bruised on the metal of his armour. He lay and thought about this, and then he found a heap of armoured men tumbling over him like clanking puppies.

He pulled himself out and to his knees, and saw the mason running in a circle screaming. He was naked, and his body smoked.

'By the bowels of the Bull,' said Vusca, standing up.

He seemed to be lightheaded. Drunk after all? He fought the urge to laugh. He lifted his hands. They were scalded. He put up these scalded hands, and touched his singed hair and brows.

The mason fell down.

Beyond, three sentries were pelting up the wall towards them.

The terrible rumbling was only thunder.

Something was on fire.

126

Something was burning there, just past the mason, between him and the running soldiers.

It was all that was left of the Pilum Commander.

'Jupiter, Father Jupiter,' moaned one of the Velites.

Vusca had the urge to laugh again. He held it down.

'It will be yours,' said the Centurion Secundo. 'Not a man here doubts it.'

Vusca did not want to seem like some blushing virgin. But he was afraid too of what had always happened in the past.

'It may be you,' he said.

'You've seen more service than I. I'm content.'

The authority would not come from Rome. There was, at the moment, power enough in Gallia to settle this. A few more days, and he would know.

The Velites carried on as if they already did know. How not, when Father Jupiter himself had made the choice? He had struck down the Pilum with his own divine thunderbolt, and left Retullus Vusca and his men unscathed but for a memento of crisped hair. (The mason, though he lived, did not count.)

The authority came at the end of the month, slipshod as things always were now, all language. But the seal was the correct one.

Vusca went out to look at his troops.

They cheered their new Pilum with willing lungs.

He was surprised. He had never thought himself popular, had been sure he was not.

His heart was in his mouth. That moment, perhaps, was the apex of his life.

Lavinia wrote him a letter, and for days he put off reading it, for she seemed only able to say, think, accomplish one thing: misery, complaints, and tears on paper were little improvement on the personal hand-to-hand variety.

Eventually he did read the letter. It was very simple.

She had been a poor wife to him. She regretted this. She wanted to go and live in the villa. If he preferred to divorce her, she acceded. On his advancement she praised him. It was only as he deserved.

He had come to realise there would be monetary complications if they divorced. Besides, he had no plan to remarry. He doubted that Lavinia had. She did not mention it.

He pondered his answer. At last, he preferred not to put anything into writing. He would go to visit her instead, at the Insula Juna. If she really was contrite, she might be quiet. Perhaps she would not cry. He could tell her she could live at the villa, he made no demands. He was sorry for her, and did not want her always on his conscience. He had not seen her for months.

In the dream, he recognised the bearded man, his kilt and oiled muscular body. They walked as if physically together along a white platform, under the leaning wall of a white building. The sky was the drum-skin sky Vusca had seen before, but smooring into darkness. Stars came out. The white glazing caught the starlight, and Vusca saw three shadows falling before them. He was astonished to cast a shadow himself, more curious as to the third. He turned to see who made the third shadow, which was of an odd shape.

No one was there.

She had done something different to the room. It looked brighter, even in that dull daylight. A bowl of purple grapes had white flowers wreathed among them; a local shawl he had never seen before was draped prettily across a couch.

Lavinia came to greet him. For a minute, he did not know her.

'How well you're looking,' he said lamely, staring.

She had gained weight. Her skin was fresh, her forearms, her throat, were rounded as they had not been since she was sixteen. The linear cuts in her face had filled out and were gone. She wore her hair a new way, not Roman, more Greek, with a ribbon across her forehead. She was not old, ten years his junior. Suddenly he remembered.

She waited on him as she had been used to do when they were first together, sending the slave away. She was very soft. She said very little. She left it all to him.

In the end he was lost for words.

Then she said, 'Do you think I've changed?'

He looked. He said, 'Yes.'

She told him why.

'I'm not a Christian any more.'

She said she had failed all the Christian precepts, although she had tried so hard. She went around with her heart withering, blaming him, blaming God. Then, on the forum, she saw a procession from the Isis Temple. That afternoon she went there. It was not, she assured him, a hive of orgiastic rites. The religion had altered. It had to do with Woman. Lavinia had found herself at the cool feet of the statue. She said that suddenly the terrible gnawing, which had been feeding on her for years, was lifted out of her. She made an offering and joined the prayers. After this, she went regularly to the temple. She had not forgotten the Christos, she said, but it was a religion she was too weak to follow. Isis, who understood, had redeemed her. She could be at peace, now.

She could let him go, now.

Vusca hesitated. Then he said, 'It isn't necessary. A divorce.'

'But Retullus,' she said, 'you have an important command. You'll want to marry again. Get children. Your name can become illustrious.'

'Who should I marry here?' he said. 'Some native girl, or a harlot?' Lavinia lowered her eyes. 'Let's leave things as they are,' he said. 'We needn't bother each other.'

'My dear,' she said, 'I'll always love you. But let

me go to the villa. Then I won't be in your way.'

He was embarrassed, but not displeased.

'Of course,' he said, 'except – why not keep here until spring? The winter's nearly on us, snow, wolves – you'll winter better in the town.'

'If you wish,' she said. She smiled. 'Whatever you say.'

Her eyes were limpid. He longed suddenly to embrace her, kiss her lips. She was the girl he had seen in the orchard, or the woman that girl had never before become.

But he did not kiss or embrace Lavinia. He stayed only as long as courtesy required. When he left, she did not cry.

The winter truly was a harsh one. The snows came sweeping down; the river froze. All night the wolves howled in the voices of lost souls that could not find the way back to Avernus.

Added to the normal duties of the Fort were the tasks of winter. The roads were kept clear, the surrounding stations open in case horses might be needed. Even during the blizzards, Dis Light unlidded its nocturnal eye.

In the Commander's quarters above the Praetorium, Vusca relentlessly attended to the business of the outpost Empire. There was no time to think of anything much beyond work.

Only once or twice he took the amethyst out of the pouch around his neck, and set it down in the brazier light, to study.

Had it changed his fortune?

Had it invited the Thunderer to strike? Had it whispered to the musing powers in Gallia until it brought him the staff of office? And had it borne Lavinia to the feet of Isis?

One twilit day, going over the bridge near the Fort gate, back from a successful winter hunt, Vusca's horse slid on the ice. He should have gone off, into the iron water, maybe under the panes of the ice itself, from which probably he would never have surfaced. But somehow neither he nor the mare fell.

He played dice now and then, with his centurions, to see. He got a reputation for winning. Perhaps they only let him.

Sometimes there were the strange dreams. He had become used to the platforms and corridors, the court above the lotus water. To the bearded man, a Semite of some variety, conceivably a priest or prince, for Vusca had seen him now both naked, and decorated in silver and jewels, a kilt with fringes, a diadem. He performed rituals at the altar in the court, or in an underground space where something towered away, dark into darkness, and only the offering fire gave any clue. Nothing spectacular or significant ever occurred.

When he dreamed of the man, the priest-prince or magician, or of the places he inhabited, Vusca went armed with memory. He knew, even asleep, he had been there before.

The dreams did not worry him, at first. Then only the recurrence disturbed him. As soon as time allowed, he meant to seek a diviner at the temple of the Father and Mother. But that winter there was not much time, except for sleep.

He did pay a few visits to his wife. His intention was to ensure she had not suffered by staying in the town, that she lacked for nothing. Sometimes he lingered. He got into the way of dining with her, of spending an evening with her. Their conversations were neutral. He spoke of the Fort and its management, or they discussed aspects of the town. He found these interludes to be comfortable, pleasing. She did her best for him. She had learned how to be gracious. They never slept together, as if such things did not exist. He preferred that. It was sex that seemed to have upset the equilibrium before, along with Christianity. Now she had Isis, and for him there were always the she-wolves. But he did not want a woman very often; he supposed that even Lililla would have palled, she had been only a novelty.

As the year turned over towards spring, and the tall clep-sydra in the Praetorium began once again to drip and to tell time, Vusca, who had been feeling a little done in, was laid up a day and a night with mild fever. He put the amethyst under his bolster, to keep it out of the way, for the Fort physician was a busy old boy.

Near morning, Vusca thought he dreamed how the amulet was made.

It was not the underground place, though it seemed the priest-prince had come from there. He was walking in the starlight back across the platform, white as the snow of Par Dis in that boiling Eastern night, that had the whiff both of marsh and desert. Together, they entered the low door, passed through the fox-run of the corridor, and came into the court of painted walls.

Going down the stair to the river, the native of the dream took Vusca with him, and gave him a first – and as it transpired, final – glimpse, through the palms, over the water, to the distant bank. Other buildings arose there, raised on platforms as was this, and one ascending in a series of terraces, a pyramid of seven steps. Huge clumps of reeds grew beneath the further bank, and something swam there, some colossal snake it looked, but the priest paid it no heed.

Leaning down, he drew up from the water a sort of basket, and in the basket lay a fish. It had been dead some while, and at a touch, its belly parted to disgorge a lilac-tinted counter.

The purpose of the fish, if it had been made to ingest the jewel, or miraculously had been caught with it already swallowed, Vusca did not ascertain.

The priest plucked the amethyst and carried it to the altar with the creatures carved around.

There the jewel was anointed with oils, beer, milk, and other liquids, and words spoken above it (a sluggish mur-muring and chanting Vusca had heard the man give vent to previously). At last the priest moved away, right against the wall, as if to become one with the paintings on it.

The jewel lay on the altar.

It lay there a long while. Then it began to glow. It was like a lilac flame, balanced on the altar stone. One flame – then three. Just above, two other lights had kindled.

In the dream, Vusca, pressed back to the wall with the priest, experienced a gust of fear. It was the correct terror of holy and profane things he had no right to witness. But he was trapped and had no choice.

What burned above the jewel were the eyes of one of the beasts carved in the altar. He could not see which it was, and did not need to. The shape was on the amulet.

The jewel blazed and the eyes of the bird-thing blazed, and there was otherwise a deepening darkness and a terrific silence that seemed to shriek.

Presently the three lights faded. As starshine returned into the court, Vusca thought he saw, for a moment, a shadow cast up against the wall, thrown by a third figure that was not there.

The fever had broken in a sweat. When he could, he shifted the amulet away from him. It felt hot from contact with him, even through the pouch.

That was the beginning of his unease.

When he came into his quarters on the third occasion and felt that someone else had recently been there, he went to the door and called the sentry in.

'Who's been here in my absence?'

The sentry looked surprised.

'No one, sir.'

Vusca's soldier's instinct, the same that had made him able once or twice to sense ambush or treachery, told him flatly that, though the sentry did not lie, neither did the ambience of the rooms. The smell was even wrong. Not of men and a man's belongings, leather, metal, papers, the charcoal and logs in the brazier. Something – almost female.

'Concentrate,' said Vusca to the sentry. 'Now.'

The sentry began to roll his eyes.

'Yes, sir. *Something*'s been in.'

Vusca crossed to the window. The glazed pane was in place and below the drop ran down sheer thirteen feet to the yard. A sentry on the adjacent tower stood alert and unmoved.

There was no explanation, and being inexplicable, it was put aside. Nothing had been damaged, there was no theft. The sense of a presence evaporated quickly.

Thereafter it would happen, or not, apparently as it chose. Once the guard on the door himself reported he had caught a noise inside, during the Commander's absence. He went to see, and investigated the two rooms, finding them vacant. He admitted that it might have been a rat or mouse. It was a kind of soft scratching he had heard, as if something clawed stole over the floor.

Vusca was tired. He awoke tired, and at night, lying down exhausted, could not sleep, hearing the trumpets through the hours till it was nearly dawn. Something nagged at him. He did not know what it was. It was as if he had forgotten some vital task. He would get up and light the lamp, and check his itinerary at the table. It was nothing to do with the Fort, this forgotten matter. It oppressed him. It never went away. If he slept he even dreamed of it (the other dreams seemed to have come to an end). He dreamed of worrying at forgetting, of trying to remember. He roused agitated, still trying. There was nothing *to* remember. He had seen to it all.

He hoped spring would lift the malaise. Spring did not. He could not consult the Fort physician, since then word would be round the barracks in half a morning, that he was sick. He visited a healer on the town's west side, who prescribed an oily draught. It made him sleep. He could scarcely wake up at all. And the nagging, the non-existent forgotten thing, went on nibbling away at him.

Something had made him take off the amethyst. He stored it in a box of bits and pieces, wrapped in its pouch.

One pale evening, as the days began perceptibly to lengthen, his Centurion Secundo, coming in to make some report, was obviously curious at finding Vusca alone. When pressed, the centurion said he had seen, so he thought, two figures at the window above the Praetorium, and meeting no one on the stair – 'Oh,' said Vusca, 'I had the soldier in from the door a moment.'

A month later, he saw it for himself. He had been waiting, in his heart of hearts, aware he was haunted. He had seen the form before. He was not startled, only afraid.

He had taken a mouthful of the healer's draught, and slept, and woke suddenly, as if at a loud cry.

But there was no noise. The room was pitch black, but for the thinner darkness of the window. And across the window passed the creature from the amulet.

It was visible for less than a second, yet it left an imprint on his sight, as on the jewel. A tall, provisionally masculine outline, but winged, clawed, and with the hook-beak head of a bird.

Vusca heaved himself up and lighted the lamp. He shook so much that he could not manage it at first. But nothing came near him, and when the light poured out the room seemed empty. *He knew it was not.* Like a child, he left the lamp to burn all night, sitting bolt upright on the bed.

And that was the beginning of his terror.

That spring Lavinia had joined the circle of initiates at her temple. This, he had to admit, as well as his position, assisted Vusca. Isis was not his goddess, but he had adequate reverence for her, which he demonstrated with a showy offering at the altar. She was depicted in decent

Roman matron's garb, a crown of corn on her head, and a
moon in her hand from which shivered drops of crystal
'tears'. After the offering, he was taken to a cell where a
priest of the upper tier received him. The man was shaven,
jaw and skull, in the Aegyptian way, nothing like the priest
of the dream.

Vusca did not prevaricate. He told the truth. A harlot had
given him an amulet, quite precious, and he had found it
benign. But latterly it had brought on some illness that
deprived him of energy, though physicians pronounced him
fit. Also, an entity was expelling itself from the stone, a
ghost, that was sometimes to be viewed, and which seemed
to become stronger as he, Vusca, weakened. The priest,
Vusca concluded, must say nothing of this to anyone. The
Commander's respect for the goddess would not prevent his
punishing an abuse of trust.

The bald priest, face like an egg, regarded him gravely.

'You may trust me.'

Then Vusca got out the amulet and put it before the
priest.

'Here. She said it was Aegyptian.'

'No,' said the priest, looking at it, not touching it. 'She
misled you.'

'I thought that was the case.' Vusca spoke, less decidedly
of the dreams. He had to fumble after them now. They had
no coherence. The priest, however, listened carefully.

When Vusca finished, the priest said, 'I must consult
another, more widely-versed than I in these things. Do you
allow me to tell him what you've said?'

'If you must.'

'Yes.'

'When shall I return?'

'Tomorrow night, before the third watch.' (Even this
temple told time by the Fort.) 'I've seen it, now take it away
with you.'

Vusca went, dissatisfied and nervous. He had not told

Lavinia the truth, only that he wished the services of a diviner, and would like to favour her own chosen temple. He thought she guessed there was some other problem.

After he had done the Night Inspection and retired to his rooms, he sat by the lamp and accepted that the presence prowled about him. Now and then, something caused the lamp to flicker, although it was a windless night. A faint aroma, like musk and blood mixed, was barely detectable. The shadow appeared plainly once, twice, against the plastered wall, where his legionary's sword was hanging, the old infantry shield, the knives, the dented breast-plate with the gouge of the axe-man's dying anger –

The shadow was, and then it was not.

The thing he found the hardest to bear was that it should be here that he was attacked, in this place which represented for him security, totality, reason – *here* –

He fell into deathly sleep at last, over the table.

The creature from the amethyst had sucked up his bad luck, and now it sucked his life. He dreamed he was with Lililla. She too sucked upon him, in that way she had taught him. He felt no pleasure but he knew he would spend his seed and she would swallow it. Her eyes were a weird dull mauve, and had no mind or soul inside them.

Three of the priests were in the chamber where he was led the second night. Lamps burned; other than a small statue of the goddess, nothing and no one else was there.

'You told me one other priest,' Vusca said.

'For this, three are necessary.'

It was pointless to practise hauteur and the Might of Rome now. He was as much at their mercy as under the surgeon's saw.

'Very well. What will be done?'

The fattest of the priests, who had a blond skin (a barbarian in Isis' order), approached him and said, in the beautiful Greek so many of them mastered: 'Commander, the amulet the woman gave you is like this: it is, as you found, benign, but then it turns. Before the first symptom, one who knew its secret would pass on the gem to another, who must accept it willingly. That is how to be free of it, to escape the turning of the energy back upon you. The woman did this. You did not know to do it. Now the time for such passage is over. We must try another course.'

'Yes.' Vusca frowned. His hands were wet and his belly griped. 'What course?'

'A casting out. A returning.'

He did not understand, but he followed their instructions. They made marks on the floor, and anointed them. One stood outside the marks, by the goddess. In an alabaster bowl he made fire. It was this priest, the one who had never addressed Vusca, who had been given the amulet.

They began to chant. Vusca did not know the words. The sounds they made, keening harmonics, droned up into the roof like mosquitoes, and set his teeth on edge.

He realised he was now more than terrified.

It was very hot in the room.

The priest who had the amulet had never touched it save through a cloth. It lay on the cloth now, before him. He spoke to it, and Vusca caught the names of Isis, and of Thot, and of Osiris. The priest sprinkled water on the cloth with the amethyst, and powders, and salt.

The ritual seemed to go on and on. All the while, Vusca felt his strength bleeding away. His head swam. It was tedious, it was horrible. He realised he had grasped already that it could not work.

Finally, bellowing something, the priest beyond the marks raised the amulet in the cloth and cast it into the fire. The other two broke from their pen and hurled things into the basin after it. An unsuitable smell of cookery rose – they had thrown in onion, and some kind of fruit.

Vusca staggered. He went down on one knee, wiping the sweat from his face. He wanted it to be over. It was useless. He would have to think of another remedy.

When the fire died in the bowl, the amulet lay there. The

heat had done something to it, meddled with its colour in some way.

He must take it, they said. Go to the Fort. They tied a knot of little cords on his arm, above the elbow. They invoked the protection of Isis.

He put a sum of money by the statue. They did not acknowledge this, aware themselves that they had achieved nothing.

The Roman commander lay down on his bed, the lamp alight, the sentry at his door.

He could not keep his eyes open. He drifted.

Vusca gripped the sword he had brought to lie beside him. The creature was not corporeal, yet maybe he could smite at it. Besides, there was a power in the sword. The power of what a soldier was. His last companion, the only one who could know everything, and would not betray –

The light fluttered and went out.

At first it was so gradual, he was not sure. It was like a constriction of the breath after too much food and wine. Only like that. But the pressure grew. It became heavier, sentient. In appalling horror he lay there, and felt the weight of the demon, crouching as the woman had done, on his loins and breast. The weight grew ever more sonorous, danker, seeping through him. He could not move. He was rigid with panic fear. And then there came the glow of two eyes, like meltings from the amethyst, hanging over him, watching him, as it sucked his life from every pore and vein and hair.

Vusca howled. By a galvanic effort, seemingly irresistible as the action of birth or death, he flung himself upward, dislodging the half-existent thing upon his chest. And as it dropped away, with the sword he cleaved it through and through, *felt* the blade go into it. But with no likeness to muscle or flesh, and not the jarring of a single bone.

When the sword ceased to penetrate anything at all, he stood panting in the darkness.

The sentry had not rushed in on him. It appeared Vusca had not even cried out as he thought he had. That was strange. Strange . . .

He held the sword, hugging it to him. Here was the last solution, after all. One way to cheat.

He sat down by the table, in the dark, with his only ally. He propped the hilt against the table's edge, the tip against his abdomen, the crucial spot, under the ribs and heart. He leaned, fractionally, on the sword's sharpness, and felt its bite like sweet consolation. 'If you're there,' he said aloud into the dark, 'I have my friend here. My friend will take me from you, if you come close tonight. Then you lose. Be warned.'

He fainted, propped there over the blade.

Barbarus came to the Fort with some display, two of his sons, and three servants.

In the room above the Praetorium, Vusca said to him, 'You had no need to be anxious. Did you think I meant to admonish you for something?'

Barbarus said smoothly, 'It is the Commander's privilege.'

'Why, have you been doing something wrong?'

Barbarus said, 'Never knowingly, Commander.'

Vusca forced a chuckle. As he had forced the coy opening gambit. Then he said, 'What have you been hearing about me in the town?'

Barbarus raised his brows. His horse-boned Gallic face was bland, moving on oiled hinges worthy of a Greek.

'Nothing?' prompted Vusca.

'Merely that we prosper under your hand.'

'And how do I look to you?'

Barbarus considered, and decided on a fact.

'Not well, Commander. There's been a lot of fever this spring.'

'It isn't fever.'

'No, Commander?'

'Do you recall, Barbarus, last summer there was a woman in the town. She had a house behind the Julian Baths.'

Barbarus paused, to let the Commander see he had forgotten all that, could only remember if reminded.

Vusca reminded him.

'I thought nothing of it, when she left,' he continued, rather archly he felt, but could not summon the requisite irritation. 'But the amulet she gave me – it's begun to work me ill.'

Barbarus had now altered. He looked like a man listening for a distant, expected shout.

Vusca added details, as many as he thought were needful. When he stopped, Barbarus, with great deference, asked a couple of questions. Vusca replied.

Barbarus said slowly, 'The Commander knows I am his slave.'

'Barbarus knows, I'm never ungrateful.'

'This is so. What may I do?'

'Is there anyone I can see who can – rid me – of this – thing – '

To his horror, Vusca found his voice was shaking, cracking like a boy's.

Barbarus ignored the cracking voice. It had not happened. He said, 'There's a man in the hills. About a day's journey in good weather – '

'He must come to me, here.'

'That may be more difficult.'

'The problem is,' said Vusca humbly, 'I find I haven't the strength, any more, to ride. Even to walk across this room is – a test.'

It was impossible to tell what Barbarus thought. You never knew. Doubtless, at any stumble they rejoiced. But they must still pretend to be sorry, try to assist, for as long as the idea of Rome remained.

'On the table,' said Vusca, 'that box. Count the coins if you like.' Barbarus bowed, tapped the box with his fingers,

did not count, since Rome was also perfect. 'Pay the man
– this healer, magician, whatever he is – pay him as you
think fit. For you, I promise you now, if – if I survive, a
talent of silver. There's a letter in with the coins to that
effect, having my seal.'

Barbarus lifted the box.

'I shall naturally destroy the letter, Commander. The
Commander's word is all that I require.'

Somehow, he lived, and did not go mad, for three more
days, two more nights. By day he oversaw the machinery of
the Fort, the drills, a parade under a burning white sun, carried out to it in a chair. He did such sedentary work as he
could, even went through an interminable itemisation of
stores with the quartermaster. Elsewhere he delegated via
his capable Centurion Secundo and various other officers.
(Was the dead Pilum sneering at him?) The men put up with
it all cheerily, and the rank and file even asked after him, it
seemed, their Old Man, laid up with the bloody fever, too
bad, and it was nice hunting weather, too.

Sometimes in the afternoons he slept. The steady diurnal
rhythms of the Fort seemed to protect him then.

The nights he was alone, alone but in company. The three
of them, himself, the demon, and the sword.

The sounds of the trumpets marking the watches were his
sanity. They were the voice of human strength and human
reason.

But he realised he did not have far to go. Barbarus' man
from the hills was the final throw of his dice. Then it would
be the sword. By the Light, he almost longed for it, now.

At sunset, on the third evening, they were sounding *gates*
and he was writing a letter to Lavinia, telling her a crippling
sickness had taken him, that he preferred the cleaner exit.
It was awkward, this letter. He had wanted to put in some
friendly, perhaps loving thing, to reward her for changing.
But he did not like the written word other than in an

itinerary or report, emotionless and exact. And the letter
read just like a report, of course. He put it aside, and then
they brought in the man.

He had been awarded a pass, through Barbarus, and
would be taken for some roving spy in the pay of the Fort.
There were genuine examples of such beings, several as tat-
tered and matted as this one, few with such crazy and wilful
eyes. Vusca thought: *When they leave him with me, he may fly
at my throat. Let him. Only another way out.*

But, when the sentry left, the man did nothing, except to
stand looking at Vusca.

It was unthinkable this ruffian could achieve anything.
The final throw had got the Dog.

Vusca was suffused by a cold and awful relief. It was
settled. He could die now.

Then the hill-man spoke, in uncouth Latin, in a scraping
voice like a flint.

'See it in he. Seeing shadow. Bird thing. All the air, *smelling* bird thing.'

A bolt of quickening went through Vusca. It brought him
back. He took hold of the table and said, 'Did Barbarus tell
you – '

'Tell. Now see. Amulet.' And more impatiently, as if with
a stupid pupil, 'Amulet! Amulet!'

Vusca took the amulet from the casket and its wrapping,
and laid it on the table in front of the hill-man. The hill-man
glanced at it. Then, he poked it with a black fingernail, and
gave off an idiot's squealing laugh. He was not afraid to
make contact, the only one who was not.

The wild eyes came back to Vusca.

'Eats you,' said the hill-man. '*Eats* you.'

Vusca shivered.

'Yes.'

The hill-man grinned.

Vusca said, 'How can I stop it – this *eating*?'

The hill-man pranced about. He said phrases in the native

jargon. Vusca caught the word for eating again. He said tiredly, 'Do you know?'

'Knowing,' said the hill-man, coming to a capering standstill. 'Eats you. You eat.'

Vusca flinched. Some part of him understood, yet he did not.

'What are you saying?'

The hill-man ignored him. He began to remove an assortment of implements, iron sticks, pincers, little bowls made of bone or shell. They all came out of his clothes.

Vusca watched as these tools of a trade were laid on the floor. In one of the dishes the man lit a flame. Then, as if it were a bit of bread, he scooped the amulet off the table. He sat down with it on the floor as though in his hut. He put the gem into a kind of clamp, and started to work on it, holding it sometimes across the little flame.

Presently mauve dusts veered off into the shell dish.

The shadows were coming down on the rooms. Night had the window, only the torches from the Praetorium to alleviate it. On the floor, the solitary flame lit the wild man's polecat face as he filed and ground away at the amethyst.

There was no sense of menace. The room seemed empty of anything that was not mortal. Was this feasible? Did the wild man have some wonderful power that held the demon in check even as he destroyed its totem?

Vusca had full understanding now. The jewel was to be powdered. Then, he would "eat" it, swallow the crystals. He had heard of physicians prescribing powdered stones, as for his grandfather's rheumatism. Even Lavinia, when pregnant, had taken some resin in molasses.

The demon had eaten Vusca's trouble, and his trouble *was* Vusca. Bad luck had made him into the man he was. The demon devoured that, and then it could go on, devouring him, down to the marrow of his spirit. Yes, he saw it now.

He was drowsy. Should he make the arrangement with the

sword? No, unnecessary yet, besides, he did not want the wild man to see it –

He heard the trumpets of the first watch. He opened his eyes and the polecat was sidling towards him out of the shadows in its draggled fitch, with a cup in its paws.

The wild man stank, much worse than any polecat. Something had screened off the smell before. Vusca basked in the new odour, of reality. One of the paw hands clutched his head, tilted his skull backward. The cup met Vusca's lip. '*Eat*,' said the wild man.

Vusca *ate*. He gulped the wine, greedily, and in the liquid he felt the crystals pass over his throat, gritty, sandy, some larger and smoother, like tasteless pills of salt.

The wild man took the cup away, and peered into it. He was satisfied and made a smacking noise with his own lips.

Vusca became marvellously, swimmingly drunk. There was nothing to be afraid of. He had consumed the consuming one. Father Jupiter! What had he done – could this be the proper trick?

He went over to the bed and lay on it.

The wine had formed a glorious warmth inside him. His entire body seemed to be feeding from it. He felt a content, an assurance he had not experienced since childhood.

The polecat came and stooped over him, and laughed filthy breath into his face. Vusca relished it. He knew, as if the gods spoke in his ear, that he had been saved. He fumbled to find money for the hill-man. The hill-man had skulked away, was going without recompense. Barbarus would see to it. Someone . . . would see to it.

The lovely night, populated only by natural things, smelling of leather, horse-hide, flowers, gently closed the Roman's eyes.

He thought: *I forgot. The sword is over there.*

He thought: *I shan't need the sword.*

Then his mind was a river of amethyst light and he went down into it to drink it up and be filled.

*

'But so many gifts,' she said. Her eyes were sparkling, she almost clapped her hands like a girl.

'I used to send you things.'

'Yes, but that was – ' Lavinia flushed and turned her head, shy of him.

She was beautiful tonight.

But then everything had a gloss and gleam upon it. Every dawn was a miracle. Dusk a blessing. Two weeks now since he had been cured. Until today he had been too cautious to be happy, with all the brightness of life summoning him. Today he had gone ten rounds, buckler and short sword, with his Secundo, in the yard. Vusca had the victory. But the Secundo, a man nine years his junior, was no faker.

And Vusca had made the offerings today. He even went down to the Greek Hercules on the forum, and gave him something. Strength for strength. The blood in him was like a young man's. Everything was better than it had been – his sight, his reach, his nerve, his brain. The accretions of the middle years were all washed off. He could begin again.

When she saw him, there in her house, she had blushed then, too. She had thought him fine. It was like the first look she ever gave him.

The orchards did not seem irremediable, overgrown and in need of pruning, but that could be done. She said she liked to be in the villa, now the summer was coming. It was really rather dreadfully run down. The window in the long atrium was broken and had been patched up with honey and wax. The heating did not work properly. There were swallows in the bath-house.

Somehow all that made it funnier, more likeable. The villa needed them. They could do things for it.

And to come out to her here, tonight, feeling as he did, free and young, that was well-omened.

When they had walked about a little, in the lavender afterglow, on which the fierce hills lay docile, like sleeping swans, they went in to the supper Lucia had set. It was a very familiar feast, the fried sausage and garlic, the basted chicken, black olives and sauce of mushrooms, the round white cheese with raisins, new bread, old purple wine from the home vineyard, and the dish of candied plums. He might have been here only a week ago, not years.

They talked about the villa and the farm. Later he went with her to the small shrine in the garden court. (The shape of the Christians' fish was gone from it.) After the offering, they sat under the colonnade, in the dark, and watched fireflies. It was what they had been used to do, in the days before their marriage. Now and then, a slave would go across the lawn on some errand. That had happened then. They had had to be furtive, then.

He began to want her, his wife, as he had wanted her long ago.

'Vinia,' he said, 'couldn't we . . .' like the young fool he had been.

But this time there was no need to dissemble or to say no.

The cries of her joy were strangers to him. Whores never raised this paean, even in pretence. He gloried in what he could do to her, and in the vigour of his own body. His seed burst from him with an overwhelming pang. He had forgotten that, too, the edge a woman's love could give to it.

They coupled twice more in the night, like hungry wolves.

In the early morning, just before sunrise, her eyes seemed vivid, flowerlike, more savage . . . husband and wife parted like lovers.

Weeks after, he said to her, 'Were your eyes always this colour?'

And she laughed at him.

It was high summer when she told him her news.

'The physician says I'll bear to term. The auspices are good. Nothing can go wrong.'

He stood with her on the hill among the plum trees. Below

the road went down to Par Dis, the cemetery, the walls.

'Isis will help me,' she said.

The curve of her belly was barely visible. In there, the life was, the son perhaps he had made. His immortality.

The other thing . . . was just a dream. (Now and then he had a slight pain, under his ribs, it was nothing, no worse than momentary indigestion. As the weeks went by, it lessened, never quite going away.)

As he rode back to the town, he kept thinking of her eyes. They had changed, as she had changed. But when he mentioned it, she told him that his eyes too had come to be another colour. And this amused them both. In the dull metal mirror he saw no alteration. Only sometimes, in the faces of men he knew well, a sudden uncertainty, a second glance –

She had a long labour, it was rough on her. But the child was flawless, and a boy.

His eyes, in the first hour he opened them, were the colour of the amethyst, might have been made from the amethyst.

Retullus Vusca, cold as death, held the life of his son in his arms. What should he do? And the impulse came to run to a high place, and there throw back this tiny breathing thing to the gods. But he only held the child, and Lavinia whispered, 'You see now, he has his father's eyes.'

It was the scar of a past battle. Let it be that. The cicatrice of a healed wound, that could no longer kill.

PART TWO

The Suicide

The prime retribution on the guilty
Is that no one can acquit himself of his own judgement.
Juvenal

Ten columns, dyed with Tyrian, marched down the cella of
the temple, to the obsidian plinth, figured with shields.
There stood the god: Mars Pater, in his armour, bearded
and helmed, night-underlit by the votive lamp. The sprays
of fig, oak and laurel from the spring festival were still
aromatic and sappy. In his small house by the shrine, the
elderly, tame wolf, sacred to the god, lay quietly, muzzle on
long paws. He was a pet of the priests, more often than not
his chain was off. He would eat from your hand, had forgotten he was ever a wolf at all.

The man who had entered, grizzled and muscular, perhaps in his fiftieth year, offered the wolf a titbit, watched
him eat, nodded, and walked back into the central aisle
before the statue.

The man carried a bundle, which he now unwrapped and
put down on the altar. He bowed his head, and seemed to
pray.

A priest came into the cella.

The man who prayed broke off, looked up; he appeared
glad that the priest was an old man, someone he had known
for years.

'Commander,' said the old priest, then smiled. 'I always
forget.'

'You forget, to please me,' said the man. 'A young puppy

149

rules the Fort of Par Dis. I'm a retired pensioner of the Empire. I tend my farm. My business is goats and vines and fruit trees.' He stopped, and said, 'And the lies I tell myself.'

The priest looked at the things which had been placed on the altar. There were three legionary javelins, three swords, some knives, the breast-plate of a cavalry skirmisher, service bracelets, bracelets for valour, the badge of command, a Medusa shield.

'The things that matter,' the man said, 'that the god values.'

'The arms of the warrior,' said the priest. 'They should hang proudly in your house. Why?'

'Because my house is ruined. There's a disease – something due to me – do you remember, I told you once – ?'

The priest's face closed like a fist. Not against the man, against the fate.

'But that was finished.'

'No. When the boy was born – I knew then. I *knew*.'

'You did nothing.'

'Nothing. I should have killed him.'

'You must speak to no one else in this fashion,' said the priest. 'There were only twenty at the Spring Rite. The priesthood outnumbers the worshippers now. These Christians have the town, as they have the Empire. The Christians are powerful, and understand nothing of this sort. Be careful, Vusca. I warn you as a friend.'

'The time for carefulness is done. Don't you see why I came here, with the offering?'

The old priest reached out and took the hand of Retullus Vusca.

'Yes, Commander. Is that all you want? Isn't there some way in which – ?'

'No, Flamen. No way but this.'

'Then, it can be arranged for you.' The priest touched the pattern of laurel on his breast, and let go the hand of the man, which was cold as winter marble. 'Your family?'

'I have – left provision, all the correct documents. But my family's cursed, Flamen. I should have seen to it. I can't. It isn't in me. A weakness. I make this sacrifice to Mars in the hope that he – '

'Hush,' said the priest, gently. 'Only the god can decide that.'

'The caterwauling of the Christos dulls all their ears,' said Vusca.

'Hush,' the priest said again. 'Come now. There's the purification. They'll make ready for you.'

'The room under the altar.'

'Yes. Come now.'

Lies and weakness. The deception of self. More than eighteen years of that, aided by them all.

The boy was handsome, his son. Everyone cherished him. He was his mother's. The women's. Vusca did not go too near. That much, at least, that distance . . . a sop to the truth. So his son grew up pampered by women, by Lavinia, and Lucia, and all the slaves. He liked the villa farm, had no hankering after a military career. At seven, Vusca had been dreaming night and day of the legions. But not Vusca's son. And Lavinia, so afraid: if he becomes a soldier he'll be sent far away. Sent away . . . something in that. Eighteen and a commission – it might be anywhere, now. It might be Rome. Vusca might send – *that* – to Rome. (Unnamed, unthought of, somewhere in his brain or heart, it stayed him.) Let the boy be a farmer, then. He was good with the land. That too was under the favour of Mars, and of Lavinia's Isis, if it came to that.

Vusca watched the boy grow up, as if from a nearby hill.

Petrus, they had called him. She had wanted the name. It had been the uncle's, popular among Christians. Vusca might have argued, but it did not seem to matter. He had no pride in this handsome son. He would say to himself that

that was because Petrus did not take after him, would not be a soldier. That made it easy.

The boy of course knew his father did not really care for him. He seemed to accept it was for the logical reason, the reason of the army. Once he had apologised to Vusca, quietly, on his fourteenth birthday. Vusca had taken the boy to the Fort, shown it to him, since that would somehow be expected. There was no doubt Petrus showed an interest. And the men took to him, the way everyone did. A father might have been able to persuade such an interested and likeable son to a taste for the soldier's life. Vusca did not attempt it. And Petrus, feeling the lack, assuming it was his fault, his omission, said that he was sorry.

When others looked at Petrus, they saw the Roman virtues. He was a beauty, but not effeminate, not soft. He was modest, friendly, reserved without coolness, dignified but ready for a laugh. The farmer's life built his shoulders and legs, he could handle a five-horse chariot with skill before he was fifteen.

When others looked at Petrus, they saw all that.

When Vusca looked at him, he saw the peculiar eyes, which others found so attractive, grey-lilac, Lavinia's. And Vusca also saw an odd birthmark, the quarter ring of tiny dark blotches around his son's collar-bone. Isis' necklace of love – that was what Lavinia called it when he was a child, kissing the marks. Women who saw them always seemed fascinated. The villa slaves had said it was something holy. Even Drusus at the Fort, who had taught Petrus chariots, had been heard to say that the broken ring was the memory of a war-scar of some forebear, carried in the blood. When Vusca looked at the marks they turned him queasy.

He had never liked to touch his son. He found it difficult to pick him up as a child. Later, if their hands brushed over some dish at table, Vusca felt a surge of revulsion, to which he never gave its actual name, and which he refused to acknowledge.

Rome still stood, like a shadow. The power of the shadow took effect. Retullus Vusca quit his command at the ordained time and went to the villa to be another farmer.

He did his best with it, the portion left to him. He had got accustomed again, quite quickly, to disappointment, to sourness. There had been that shining space, less than a year, in the centre of his life. It died down like a fire and left him with the used-up charcoal, which crumbled and had no heat.

There were no other children. He did not sleep with Lavinia after the boy was born. Latterly he did not want women.

Then there was the day in the orchard.

It was the start of harvest, the fields full of men, and the pickers busy with the fruit. At noon, activity fell off. He sat polishing one of the swords by the trough, with the dog at his feet – and then the dog growled very low, and got up and went away, and his son came through the sunlight and the trees. It was curious that, the way the dog never took to Petrus. Vusca's dog, perhaps it had caught Vusca's allergy. Vusca thought of a recent incident with the horses hired by Petrus for the chariot, some trouble – then Petrus was in front of him. The sun was behind his head, giving him a sun god's halo, dampening down the shade of his eyes.

'Father – '

'Yes?' The false jovial voice came out pat, the tone which held Petrus firmly off.

'Father, can I speak to you?'

'Why not?'

His son – he was sixteen, a young man now – uninvited did not sit. He said, as if searching in a barrel for the words: 'Mother's going to talk to you. She's been going on about it. A marriage.'

Bored (and under the boredom the aversion rising in him like sickness). 'Well, if you want,' said Vusca.

'I don't, sir. I don't want to marry.'

'You've heard the girl's ugly.'

'No. I think she's supposed to be all right.'

'Too old?'

'Only twelve.'

'That's nothing then. She's young enough to train. Oh, I know who your mother has in mind. A decent family, with Roman blood. You might as well. Out here, choices are limited.'

'I don't want to marry, sir.'

'Wait,' said Vusca. 'What are you saying?'

'Never,' said Petrus.

'Some vow?' Vusca scowled. He wanted to feel an ordinary emotion. It was coming, if he tried. Normal annoyance. A son who would not breed. 'Or do you have the Greek ailment? You like your own gender best? You'll grow out of it. Have you never had a woman?'

Under this ballista strike, Petrus went very white. The pallor threw up the colour of the eyes. Suddenly they were brilliantly in evidence.

'Not – not what you said. And I've never had a woman, no. Father – I'm afraid to do that.'

Vusca laughed. He looked away from the eyes, down the orchard. 'Yes, you're not the first coward there. Believe me, it's not any punishment. You'll like it. Only virgins can be tiresome. You'd better get in some practice first. Go to the *She-Wolf.* The other places aren't worth – '

'*No* father. I don't mean any of that. I *can't.*'

Vusca was exacerbated, embarrassed. (Something in him said, Don't let him speak. Don't hear him out.)

'What about your friend Drusus? Hasn't he – '

'Father, I've never even – once, it started – and I couldn't – I knew if I did – something horrible – it was like falling out of my body, swallowing and choking – '
Petrus was no longer rational. His voice was high and hysterical, like a girl's.

Vusca stood up. He pushed his son away from him.

'You spend too much time with your mother. Go to a harlot and tell *her* all this. Let her put you right.'

He walked away and left Petrus by the trough.

What should I have done then? Heard it, and *known* it. I should have held him in my arms and told him, because I could have reasoned it, could have seen through the flimsy veil. I should have loved him like my son, that he was, and had the courage, with the enemy at our gate, to speak the truth and run him through. By the Light, he knew, he *knew*. Not knowing, and knowing it all. He only came to me for the answer. He would have made the sacrifice. *He was my son.*

Vusca knelt in the cell under the altar.

The purification was over. They were bringing him the wine, now. He needed the wine. He was so cold.

He could not weep, his whole life had taught him steel, not water.

The marriage came two years later. The same girl, fourteen by then. The family had waited, for Vusca's name was reckoned on. The girl brought a small house with her dowry. It was in the town, near the Baths of Mercurius, a poor area going generally to hovels. There seemed to be a reverse of the arrangement between Vusca and his wife: Petrus installed his bride in her town house, and kept to the farm. He only brought her there when for propriety he must.

She was a pretty girl, a blonde with dark Roman eyes, and all the Roman ways studiously ingrained in her. Though she was a Christian, she also worshipped the other gods at their festivals.

At first she seemed merely nervous. Eventually it was obvious she was unhappy. At some point, about a year after the wedding, she confided to Lavinia that Petrus had never slept with her. She was still a virgin. She thought it was her

fault, that she smelled, or that he despised her barbarian blood. (Vusca only heard of all this later.) Lavinia reassured the girl, and took her to the Isis temple, where they procured some draught or other, an aphrodisiac.

Whatever the plan, it was carried out while the girl was still staying at the farm. She wanted Lavinia's approval and support, and perhaps to boast of success.

Vusca was off with a couple of the men, hunting. The woods to the north were full of boar that season, though they did not have any luck. They were away five days.

They returned one late afternoon, coming along the west road with the sun behind them. The villa looked as usual, the fields ripening, smoke going up from the bath-house. Then, getting closer, Vusca saw no one was out in the fields or the orchard, that the smoke was not from the bath-house vent, but from a burning strip on the slope beyond. He sent two men running to deal with that and rode fast for the villa.

The slaves and field-workers were clustered in the outer compound. They parted before him and could not seem to find any voices when he shouted at them. Then a mad screaming started in the house. It sounded like a woman in labour. The slaves made signs against evil.

Vusca ran into the building. His actions were horribly prepared. He was not amazed, or alarmed, there was only depression, a sense of futility and defeat.

Lavinia dashed into his arms. She said that in the night Petrus' wife had gone mad. She had begun to shriek, and done so intermittently ever since. She had also torn herself with her nails. They had had to tie her to her bed. Petrus, who had been with her, had vanished. A window was shattered and there were marks on the wall. Lavinia believed a murderer had got in and killed her son, carrying off the body. This was what had driven the girl insane. Far-fetched as it was, what other explanation could be possible? (She did not admit to the story of her

son's sexual reticence, the aphrodisiac, until three days after.)

Vusca went to see the wife of Petrus.

Lucia watched over her, in apparent terror. The girl was trussed. Her body, partly bare, showed deep bleeding scratches, but her nails had never been long, these were more like the scoring of a bone pin. She screamed and tossed, then fell slack until another fit of screaming and tossing came over her. She had forgotten speech. The window had been covered now, for it seemed the sounds of pigeons flying by made her worse.

There was a faint odour in the room, something like poultry.

Vusca found that he had gone near the bed, and was staring into the eyes of his son's wife. They had a curious glaze on them. Then she screamed and screamed and her tongue poked out like a lizard's.

Retullus Vusca had the wine now, in the room under the altar of Mars Pater. He drank it slowly, longing for the warmth, which did not come.

He thought dimly of the time which followed his son's disappearance. Was it only now that it seemed to have such a preordained progression?

How they had searched, and not found. How the screams had flickered out in the shuttered room, and the girl who was Petrus' wife became silent and heavy and pliant like a piece of dough. The day when they knew she was with child. When he first saw the new colour of her eyes, like lotuses in a marsh.

How he heard of a demon in the woods. How a native man was killed and a native girl was raped by something among the trees. How *her* eyes looked, and *her* belly began to swell.

How Retullus Vusca began to go hunting, and when he went away in the twilight of the dawn, not after boar any

longer, he saw the lotus eyes of Lavinia watching him from a window.

And when he slept in the woods, he saw the eyes in his sleep, all those eyes made from the amethyst, and waking and lifting his hunting knife he looked and saw the same eyes there, reflecting in the blade.

How he hunted over the hills, above the native hutments, in the woods, going always further and further from the town, the shadow of Rome, and reason.

He wondered if he would discover the polecat man from the hills, who had done this. He did not think he would. Barbarus had died years back of a stomach sickness. But Vusca too kept the small pain under his ribs, the scar of the battle he had not, after all, won –

The woman from the hutment gave birth before term, to a monster. Evidently they killed the baby, which was scaled. The mother died, or they helped her die. Then Petrus' wife started her labour.

As Vusca was in the atrium collecting his spears and knives for hunting, Lavinia entered. Her hair and robe were loose in the early morning. She smiled and said, 'Don't go.' She had not smiled since Petrus' "murder". Now she took Vusca's hand from the knife and put it on her breast. A flare of lust went through him. For years he had not gone with any woman. Now he engorged, and in her starving smiling purple eyes he saw the reason.

'Get away from me,' he said. 'It isn't you, you bitch, don't you know that yet? How we are – what's in us, with our blood?'

She shook her head, she rubbed herself against him. He went past her, and out of the villa. His dog, which had been running up to him, turned suddenly back with a whine.

'*Good*, Remus,' said Vusca. 'Good dog, brave lion. Yes, that's right. Stay away.' And the dog wagged its tail, trembling.

Vusca leaned on the wall until nausea and darkness subsided.

Then he went towards the hill country.

He realised, almost too late, his error. Or perhaps the god – Mars the Warrior, Mithras, Bringer of Light – perhaps the god told him.

He turned back, got on the road, and reached the town gate before sunset.

Only the whores of the west town now went to the Baths of Mercurius; the deity was their patron, they had some claim. Behind, a plethora of huts had gone up, among mud alleys where once a garden grew. There had been some talk, in a wine-shop, some killings, orgiastic and bloody, the fanatic work of some fresh sect . . . the women went out in pairs.

The house of Petrus' wife stood by a ruined shrine, and a great castanea shaded the doorway, while it wormed roots like levers under the wall.

The decrepit slave who kept the door knew Vusca, and let him in. The slave had forgotten, or else did not know, asking after the young master and his wife. Vusca grunted some falsehood. He inquired if the house stayed quiet. The slave said it did, but he was deaf and almost blind. The other slaves had been taken over to the villa or reclaimed by the girl's family.

The ancient slave brought candles, and bread and wine for Vusca's repast, then crept off to his quarters on the upper floor.

Vusca ate, and inspected his hunting weapons. Then he doused the light.

Even here, over the quiet night, he could make out the trumpets from the Fort. He had not heard them for a long while. *Gates*, and the first and second watches. Then there was some clatter from a nearby brothel that cut other sounds off from him. He resented that. He visualised the drunken party, the men topped up with lechery and the whores loud with beer, the bad musicians, all the stuff of a paltry world that he had looked down on and which now he nearly envied.

The party guttered and went still at last. An owl cried over the roofs of the town. The dining room, where the slave had taken him, looked on the garden court (weeds and a cracked urn) and he saw the stars, and the opposite roof over the colonnade and vaguely the stars darkened and the tiled roofs, the pillars, the urn, came clear. An hour to *cockcrow*, dawn. And something was moving on the tiles there, *something* –

Vusca sat in his shadow like stone. What was on the roof? He thought of the owl, the wide wings, a dart of a head – then it was gone.

In the stillness, sharp as a needle, Vusca heard the noise of something inside an upper room across the court.

It was not the slave. The slave slept at the other end of the house. It did not sound like the slave, either. It lightly shuffled, and hopped.

Vusca gripped one of the spears. The knife was in his right hand.

He went to the place where the stair was, and climbed up sightless, silent, to the second storey. He heard the noise again at once, behind a door, a bird's noise, scuttering and pecking about.

He felt nothing now. His heart raged, but he was numb, as if from poison.

He opened the door, and pushed it, and went through.

It was a room without furnishing, save for some old sacks. A window showed grey sky, and the other way in.

Under the window something was feeding. It glanced up, and a coil of black tissue trailed from its mouth back to the torn-out human heart that lay before it. The mouth was not a mouth, but the beak of a gigantic bird. The eyes shone, two mauve stars came in with it at the window.

Vusca knew it. He knew it for the demon on the amulet, and also he knew it for his only son. Then he plunged forward, kicked it down, crashed upon it, and drove the knife through its left eye into the mindless brain beneath.

The hands and arms held him in a desperate embrace as it died. It was the only time Vusca had been held in the arms of his son. When they let go, the creature was stretched under him, the beak open and the remaining eye glaring.

Vusca stood up. He felt neither triumph nor grief, only an awful freezing coldness. For a time he stayed there, aimless, and the sun started to come and *cockcrow* sounded miles away. The dreadful thing, the worse thing was, he did not know what to do.

It was broad day when he thought of something. He could detect the slave creeping about below by then, and sparrows twittered in the garden court.

Vusca rolled the body of Petrus into a corner, among the sacks. Then he struck fire, and gave the room to it.

When he was sure the flames had hold, he went down and collected the slave, explaining to him that the house was burning. The slave sobbed as they went into the street. Soon a crowd collected, and watchmen came running to tackle the blaze. Vusca got away easily in the confusion. Probably they would save most of the house, but not the upper room. Petrus had had his funeral pyre. He had even had tears, though they were the tears of a slave, and shed in ignorance.

He did not go back to the villa. He sent a man, discovered in a tavern, a former legionary who had served under him, and was known to Lavinia, to fetch the shield and breastplate and swords. The man was an habitual drunkard, but could be trusted in the morning, if offered money. That was what the *Auxilia*, the legions, had become. He told the man to ask after his son's wife.

When the fellow returned he had had a drink or two, but carried all the gear in an untidy bundle. He grumbled, not bothering as to why it was wanted, said he had had nuisance with Vusca's slaves who seemed to think thievery was afoot. There had been another murder, in the native slum over the river – the heart of the victim was missing. And there had been a fire at Vusca's son's house on the west side, did Vusca know? Vusca said he had heard.

'And my daughter-in-law?'

'Ah that,' said the soldier, '*two* of 'em. A fine boy, and a little girl. Now maybe you think that calls for a cup of wine?'

Vusca paid him and gave him his wine, and left him in the tavern.

Vusca went out carrying his nondescript bundle, wrapped in the old army cloak.

He had prayed she would die, and the progeny would die too.

Now he should go to the villa after all, go with the knife, see to it. Simple, to kill a child with amethyst eyes. But he knew he could not.

He sat on a stone bench in the street, near to a baker's. All the town passed him, the carters and loafers, the powdered girls with their attendants, a Christian priest, a sweating bricklayer who asked him to move his feet and said, when he did, 'Thanks, dad.'

Vusca sat all day on the bench. No one knew him. He was some old worn-out dad to this town where he had lived his manhood and commanded the Fort and walked the arrogance of Rome into the streets.

When it was dark, the whores began to call from their lamplit doors.

He shouldered his life and his soul, and went to the temple of Mars.

He had finished the priests' wine.

Only death could warm him now.

Retullus Vusca, purified for the act by an elder priesthood, took up the sword. He drove it in through the abdomen, upward, leaning into the agony to meet the point, until it bit into his heart. Then he rested. The stroke had been exact. He need do nothing more. He was not afraid. He did not mind the pain, which was already flowing out from him. A tender warmth blossomed where the pain had been, on the blade in his heart.

It was then he discovered the final task still to do. By the miracle of the sword cut, a warning had been left to him, under his hand, to give – somehow he must achieve it.

The Roman crawled over his blood to the spot where the Medusa shield leaned on the wall. Through the nothingness of death, he struggled to see and feel her wounded face.

He prayed for an impossible strength. The god heard him.

As he fell back on the floor of the cell, Vusca dragged the shield with him. It covered him against the cold and dark. He could sleep now.

THE GREEN BOOK

eyes like emerald

PART SIX

The Madman

My apprehensions come in crowds;
I dread the rustling of the grass;
The very shadows of the clouds
Have power to shake me as they pass.
Wordsworth

Because it was obvious he was mad, the crowds in the market made way for him. Only when he seemed likely to prove difficult did they shove at him, though once or twice urchins, and others nearly as or more unfortunate than he, pelted him with clods of dung and small sharp pebbles off the ground. Formerly, he might have been well-dressed, fashionably got up. Now the doublet was unlaced, half the points ripped out, the shirt filthy and torn, and he had lost a shoe. His hair was matted. Some said he had been come on sleeping or swooned among the pig-pens, like a regular prodigal. Even those that attacked him were wary, however, for he was young, and strong in his body. He might have been handsome, but for the affliction, and a curious film across his dark eyes.

Near the area where the pig market gave on the Dyers Street, a commotion ensued. A bird-seller was coming down with his wares in their cages strapped on all over him, and met the madman with twenty paces between them. Instantly every bird in its cage went wild, fluttering and cheeping, dashing itself on the wicker bars. The bird-seller tried vainly to quiet his charges. Seeing the madman, too, he nervously pressed back and invited him to pass. The lunatic, though, appeared smitten with weird fright. He fell against a wall, and beat his fists on his head. Then, with a shout, he ran straight at the bird-seller and felled him. The man went down hard at the impact and some of his cages were splintered and the panic-struck birds sprayed up into the sky. The madman meanwhile ran roaring up Dyers Street, where a few came out and pursued him, thinking he was a robber making off with something.

He was lost again in the alleys on the west side of the markets.

Raoulin, said a voice in his head, *you must go at once to the university*.

No, he answered. *No*.

In the courtyard of the Sachrist, the grave tutor led them in a discussion in the Platonic mode, but a girl stood under the colonnade, with a skull in her hands. Blood dripped from her skirt. The master indicated her. 'Here we view the progress of corruption.' And her flesh slid from her bones. Only a skeleton at last, holding in its latticed hands the second skull.

The madman sprang up from his bed of refuse under the ruined wall, and ran away.

Images hunted him through the alleys of Paradys like dogs. He would race until he went down, and then they were on him.

Even as he ran, he heard their belling behind him.

Raoulin, said the voice. *Raoulin*.

Yes, he said. But he did not know who Raoulin was.

Find a priest, said the voice.

He had sinned, and would die unshrived.

For some priests had already passed him, going up to the cliff of the colossal Church. They told their beads and murmured as they walked, unaware of anything beyond them in the world. Only one, younger than the rest, glimpsing the madman, quickly crossed himself and looked away.

What could he say to a priest?

I, a poor sinner . . . I lay with the dead. My fault, my great fault.

*

In the night, he travelled aimlessly, an escaped beast that takes the City for the jungle, and so cannot comprehend it. Down along the quays he rambled. The rats watched him as he drank from the dirty river. Under the water he saw a corpse go by, her hands clasped at her bosom, her hair brushing his drinking lips.

Near where some ships were moored with swags of sails across their broad arms, a fire was alight on the stones. Men sat dicing and he slunk closer, attracted to some forgotten code of fellowship.

Presently the men were aware of a presence.

'Something's out there.'

'A dog. Can smell our dinner broiling.' (This could have been true, for Raoulin had noticed that meat and spices cooked over the fire in a pot.)

'Doesn't the scripture say, as you do even to the least of my brothers?' asked another man, and digging in the pot with his knife, he took out a bit of meat, and threw it away into the dark where Raoulin was.

The other men cursed him. The benefactor cursed them louder.

Raoulin gnawed the meat down to the bone. But when he reached that bone, his gorge rose, he flung the bone from him and ran away from it, into the jungle tangle of the night.

In the hour before the summer dawn, two women went by the broken shed he had found to lie in, sweating and tossing and dozing, and they heard his sounds, and glanced as they crossed the doorless door. They were two harlots from the quays, who plied there dusk to dusk.

'Well,' said the taller girl, 'there's one won't be wanting our comfort.'

And they laughed in the way of women who have nothing on earth to find amusing, and can therefore be amused by anything.

When they were gone up the shadowy path, Raoulin shuffled to the shed's opening. He had an idea, a want, to go after. No sooner did he feel this, and act on it, than his mind was wonderfully swept clean. No images or thoughts or voices started up to appal him. With a blissful singleness of purpose, he climbed behind the two women.

In a brief while he saw them before him again, outlined in the black by some vagary of night-sight that had come to him.

They did not converse, and walked sluggishly, doggedly. Then one hesitated, and turned to look back with a gleam of her pale face.

'Something is behind us.' The tone was not amusement but dread, now.

'Oh you and your night fancies. Three years you've worked the bank with me, and you still see ghosts.'

'I saw its eyes. Green, like a cat's. But up in the air.'

The other turned then. She stared at Raoulin, and did not apparently make him out at all.

'There's nothing. If there was, they'll want the same as the others. Charge twice for a ghost.'

They went on, and Raoulin continued after them, though hanging back rather more. Instead of the roiling abyss within him, now he knew a dim excitement. It was not hunger or thirst, nor lust, yet it was something, a need that was undeniable, though nameless.

In an impoverished street whose tops bowed together, the harlots parted. The scared girl flitted away under an arch. The other pushed open a door and went into the night hole beyond.

There was no bolt or lock to the door. It was simple to steal upon it, to peer in at the crack.

The girl had lit a candle, which made a huge light in the nothingness. Raoulin saw her like a cameo, white on umber. There was another, too. A man unbeautifully asleep on a pallet, who at the light sat up and snarled, 'Is that you? What have you got?'

The harlot took out a few coins from her sleeve and let them fall into his hand.

'Is this all? You're not keeping anything back, slut-face? I'll – '

'I know what you do if I try to cheat you. And it's harder, my work, with bruises.'

'Well and good. Now take a penny and go out and get me a pot of ale.'

'Sweet Jesus. At this hour? It's almost morning and haven't I been out all night – '

The man rose up and slapped her glancingly across the head.

'Stop your nagging. Do as you're bid.'

The girl palmed the penny and came suddenly back to the door.

No one was there as she stepped outside, but as she began her trudge towards the tavern, something did appear, like a greater shadow thrown up at her back, with, near the apex, two narrow green incandescences.

Eastward, over the heights and scoops of the City, the sky was draining of its black. The creatures of Hell, which preferred darkness, would be seeping down into the ground.

Years ago, when she was only a brat of five, there had been atrocities committed in the dark. Her own mother, a whore before her, had sat whispering over the cooking fire with her cronies, all telling each other of the woman by the fish market who had had all her parts torn out. And the body was burned, for they said a devil had done it and evil's infection might be there on the rags of the corpse. That thing, certainly, had toiled by night at its ripping, as she and her sisterhood toiled against posts, trees, and walls, or flat in some leaky boat under the wharf.

These were the thoughts in the trudging girl's head. She

put them aside briskly and promised herself a swig of the stink-pig's ale.

As she was turning aside into Goat's Alley, the harlot realised that a man was behind her. She could smell him, and feel his heat, and next moment he caught her round the body.

'Hey, hey,' said the girl, who was used to rough embraces, and she turned herself to look.

Her first impression frightened her, for the alley was still all of the night, and what she seemed to find had hold of her was a black shape, maned, and with teeth drawn, luminous-eyed, uncanny.

But she sloughed the notion, and stared, and saw instead the sick beggar from the shed-shelter.

He was shaking with a fever, hot with fires, and his eyes, if they were not demoniac, had a rabid glare she knew to be careful of.

'Now what can you be wanting, sieur?'

His teeth glittered as he panted. He seemed to try to force her to the wall.

'Not now,' she said, 'my old man's waiting. And you're not fit for it.'

To Raoulin her voice was barely audible, and she herself seemed a great way off down a tunnel of mists and lights. It seemed he must have her, carnally. His loins had readied themselves, and so after all this had been the want which drove him to hunt her down. And yet, the want was not solely lust, as he had known it was not, in its parched starvation, a hunger or thirst. His entire body strained towards a sort of stretching and yawning, and the picture in his mind now was of a snake yawning off over its head its entire skin.

But the girl resisted, playful and determined.

She seemed scared now, too, like the other one.

'If I call,' she said, 'Jenot will hear me at the inn. He's a big man. He'll come and see to you. Now leave off.'

She thrust at him and Raoulin slammed her into the wall.

At that she did scream, and the cry brimmed through his brain. He saw himself, as if from the air above. He saw himself – and another.

A corpse-light was over him. It was in his eyes. It altered him. This one could throw the girl back and rape her. At the crisis, the stem of flame would mount through him, as he had seemed to feel it before, from phallus to sacrum, through the vertebrae, into the skull. And then –

And then the demon which possessed him, which he had conceived at his union with the dead girl – the demon would yawn off his skin and make him, as it had made Heros d'Uscaret, into the mindless, feeding unlife which was *itself*.

Raoulin, by an effort of flesh and will, wrenched himself from the terrified whore. He seemed, as he did so, torn apart. Nausea boiled in his guts, he went blind with pain and illness, and staggering away, left her. She ceased yelling at once, and let him go. No man came rushing to her aid, either. The alley was empty. And the next. Not that he saw.

He tried to pray to God. No words would come. He had mislaid all the orisons, all the entreaties.

But what he had almost done, to her, to himself –

It came to him he had been hearing her thoughts, those memories that concurred with Helise's tale, and that might be the prelude to the latest tale, the rebirth of the demon.

In the nightmare he had no compass points. There was nowhere he might return, no sanctuary to be had. Friends, family, the swamps of raptures, the pinnacles of debate and learning – nowhere could he perceive salvation.

And he recalled how an elderly stern sour priest had warned him of the loose women of Paradys, of some dire disease he might catch. But he had caught the contagion of the Devil.

The sky was bright now, over his left shoulder, where Satan stood in the stories.

Then the last alley broke into a slender street that passed under some tall houses. One had a vine growing up its timbers. He gazed at it, as if at a creeper from Atlantis. Then his legs gave way. He fell in the street. He lay there, and heard the world start to be industrious all about, the notes of brooms and pans, a donkey's complaint, a young girl singing. The Prima Hora was sounding from a score of churches.

Raoulin scrabbled in his belt, obscenely, as he would have brought forth the blade of procreation and death. This blade was better. Strange he had not recollected, until now, the break of day, his knife.

As he found the place between his ribs, and poised the steel there, an insane whirling and denying dashed through his blood. Suicide was the ultimate sin. (Did he think God would ever forgive him? Through the endless centuries until Doomsday, Heros had said, He would not.)

'It's you,' said Raoulin, 'foul thing, tempter. You can't dissuade me.'

Raoulin did not credit God, besides. The Devil had won. But in this one game he should not.

Raoulin jammed the knife between two ribs, for the heart.

The pain was incredible. Bile and blood came into his mouth. He wept, and pushed the blade in further.

His heart seemed to break, like a pane of glass.

A woman was coming down the street with a pitcher, for some well. She was like an apparition. He saw her halting to consider him.

Before he saw what she would do next, night dropped back on him. Down into Hell he rolled head over heels.

PART SEVEN

The Demon

So runs my dream: but what am I?
An infant crying in the night:
An infant crying for the light:
And with no language but a cry.

Tennyson

They were respectful to her, in the City streets, when they saw her now and then going to and fro with her nurse or her maid. They said, she had been educated like a boy, could read many languages, was fluent in Latin, had knowledge of music and ritual dance old as time . . . which was charming, and of alchemy . . . which was unsuitable. They did not suggest she was a sorceress, as they never plainly referred to her father as a magician. But they did call her, in general parlance, the Beautiful Jewess.

She had risen very early, and gone to pluck herbs in the house's inner courtyard; these seen to, she sat reading a treatise of Galen's, there in her bedroom which caught the morning sun. Her black hair hung about her like clusters of black grapes, and covered only by a little black velvet cap. The striped cat, now a matron of the establishment, lay playing with a sunbeam on the bed. Even the doll remained, seated in a corner on a wooden chest, a toy no longer, but venerable.

There came a noise from the street. The Beautiful Jewess raised her head, and the cat paused, open-mouthed.

The noise was not especially usual. It seemed to be that of a dropped pot, which shattered.

The very next instant, someone knocked on the street door.

Ruquel's window looked east, into the court. Even the sound had reached her by a sideways trick, vision was not possible.

Yet something caused her to get up, touching the cat upon the forehead as she went by (rather as the *mezuzah* was touched at the doorway) and out of the room and down the stair.

In the hall below, Liva the porter had already unfastened the door. He was almost seven feet tall, mild as a lamb, but evidently capable of killing with his bare hands. He had come to the household several years since.

The nurse was also at the door, and outside a throng of women and a few men had gathered. There had been exclamations. Now a silence. Into this, Ruquel descended.

The nurse, seeing her, made a motion she should not approach.

'Why not? What is it?'

The nurse put her hand over her own eyes. Though she was protective, she knew Ruquel had not been trained to docility, or ignorance. 'An awful sight. A young man has slain himself at our door.'

Ruquel stopped a moment, very pale and straight, then she came down the last of the stair and crossed the hall. Liva too gave way to her in the door.

He lay, the suicide, with no doubt across the very threshold, as if the angel of death, in a passover, had thrown him there. His black hair streamed on the cobbles, his face had been calmed by the darkness of his sleep, all but the eyes. Closed, they had about them a strange tension, as if he had been weeping. One seemly thread of blood ran from the corner of his mouth. His hand rested quite gracefully and couthly on the hilt of the knife, which otherwise was sunk into his breast.

Ruquel regarded him. The watchers observed the Beautiful Jewess went whiter than her own whiteness. Then she knelt down, and put her fingers to the temple, the throat, of the cadaver. Then she set her hand in the air over his lips, and brought it away.

After a minute, she lifted her long-lashed eyes and announced: 'Liva, you must bring him into my father's house. He isn't dead.'

Someone in the street protested. Ruquel did not take notice, but as Liva was leaning forward, Ruquel touched his arm, and said quietly, 'Take care as I did to have no contact with the blood.' Without a question Liva nodded. He leaned and gripped his burden, the weight of a full-grown man, like that of a child.

Ruquel rose. 'You know that my father has tutored me,' she said to the street. 'The muscle in the young man's chest is very hard, and he, it seems, very weak. He could not complete the blow.'

When the door was shut, the nurse said, 'If he lives, they'll say your father, or you, raised him from the dead.'

'So be it,' said Ruquel, with an abstracted smile.

Haninuh, when he returned from an excursion into the City that twilight, was met by his daughter at the door. Though the house was always well lit, it was the hour of lamp-lighting, and Ruquel presented to her father a poetic oriental image as she stood before him, limned by the ivory candle-lamp she bore, in her silver earrings and little velvet cap, and barefoot as about the house she always was. The striped feline sounded its timbrels at her side.

'Welcome, my father.'

The rite of homecoming was performed swiftly but warmly.

'You have a guest,' she said then. 'We housed him in the Cedar Chamber.'

'Oh, does he have a liking for trees?' (The chamber was painted over one wall to the ceiling with a cedar tree; some guests had declared they heard all the owls and doves of Lebanon mewing in its branches.)

'He likes nothing, being nearly dead.'

Haninuh frowned. 'He's a man of the City?' This was a Jew who never spoke of "gentiles".

'I have not seen him before. If my father has seen him, how can I say.'

But she revealed, as they climbed the stair, the morning's astonishment, passing on to the afternoon's labour. In an interpolation, she stressed the care she had felt prompted to take with regard to bodily fluids, the protections she had formed. She was very skilled herself in medicines, for the Jew himself had taught her, and in other elements more mysterious.

'Will he live?' asked Haninuh therefore, in the corridor.

'It's for my father to say. I trust he will.' Ruquel turned her candle from a draught, and her face was veiled in shadow. 'But, he longs to die.'

'Why so, I wonder? You name him a young man, and sound but for the wound.'

They reached the door of the Cedar Chamber. Inside, a lovely lamp of Eastern filigree hung from a stand and dusted the air with frankincense. The great tree spread over the plaster, and the nurse kept watch in its shade. In his bed, bathed and made clean, the suicide lay on his pillows, like a saint of wax.

The Jew went to a basin and washed his hands. He spoke inaudible words. Then he proceeded to examine the unconscious man thoroughly. At length, he straightened up and replaced the covers.

'He gives little enough sign of life. But life persists. Rarely have I seen such a wound seal itself so rapidly. I know your cleverness as a doctor, Ruquel, but from what you tell me, this is not so much your wisdom as some connivance in the flesh. Spirit and body are at odds.'

Later, when they took their supper together, the father questioned the daughter over again, and they discussed their visitor broodingly.

'How is it, finding him thus, you thought he might survive?'

'I hoped for it,' said Ruquel simply. 'At first I could find no tremor of the heart. But at my touch it came as if to meet me. And then seemed to grow stronger.'

'I cannot think he and I have been familiar with each other,' said the Jew, 'yet there's about him something I know or imperfectly remember. Well. Until he wakes, speculation bears no fruit. Before you sleep,' he added, 'if you're willing, go to the room and make music on your harp.'

'Your will is mine,' she said.

'And am I to think,' he said, 'you do it only to please me?'

The harp which Ruquel brought to the Cedar Chamber was a model of the little *kinnor*, a crescent of bow-horn which she leaned to her shoulder, from which crescent ten horsehair strings stretched to a horizontal bar of ereb willow. Beneath, the unstretched tails of the strings provided a fringe that, occasionally, the striped cat was wont to bite.

The nurse nodded in her chair. Liva was soon due to take his watch.

Ruquel sat where she could see the mosaic of the filigree lamp upon the sick man's face.

She plucked chords of a twanging fluidity from the harp, and, as the music found its way, sang very low a melody without words, old as the Jordan, perhaps.

She had serenaded him for less than three minutes when a sigh, more a convulsion, rushed in and out of him. His eyelids fluttered and one arm sought from the covers. (The nurse slept on.)

Ruquel did not stop her music, but now her eyes were fixed only on him.

The wordless song flowed and twined among the reedy pangs of the harp.

Another three or four minutes elapsed.

Abruptly, with no further prologue, the eyes of the young man opened wide.

Ruquel ceased playing and singing.

She was intensely unnerved, as if fire had been thrust into her face.

She had known that his eyes would be dark as her own. But the eyes looked at her now. Focused on her with feral acuity. They were brilliantly, violently and unhumanly green. Emeralds set in optic sockets.

Mastering herself, Ruquel said, 'Sieur, you're with friends. Lie quietly. I shall fetch my father.'

But the young man said, 'It hears the music. It knows your song.'

'Who?' said Ruquel, holding back her terror with a rein of steel.

Then he sagged into the pillows, and he only said, 'My God, my God. Didn't I die? It's all to do over. If you're kind, fetch your father, someone, to brain me with a mace. Then burn – then burn the body.'

Raoulin slept the slumber of opiates. In that deep sea, he lost himself, and coming back to shore learned a month of days had been sunk there too. He did not protest. In sleep he had been incapable of harming another, or of facilitating – *that*, which was now his constant companion, the unborn child of death and destruction caged in the male womb of his loins.

Somewhere in the sleep there had been dreams. He recalled none of them, and was glad of that. Sometimes, also, he believed Haninuh the Jew had questioned him, and he had answered. And perhaps *it*, too, had done so. And he seemed to have heard the soft jangle of the *kinnor*, then, across dark reedy waters under a lion moon.

There came an evening, when Raoulin had returned from the places of drugged sleep, and he was shown his body, a little emaciated, but with the wound healed to a plaited line. If he should move suddenly, then the muscle quirked and pained him, that was all.

The strong man came and lifted him, and the woman washed him and he was fed. There were some days of that, and some nights of shallow dozing, for sleep had been too long with him and now proved elusive.

He was afraid they would let the beautiful daughter in to tend on him. He was afraid of what the demon would make him do. And of the aftermath.

But the daughter did not come near him now.

There began to be days of letting him out to walk in a small enclosed court with fruit trees in pots, and herbs and flowers and a little sunken well. One day, as he marched aimlessly about there, to toughen himself – because they had said he must – he beheld a striped cat, which arched its back and hissed at him, then jumped up a series of perches to a window above, where it vanished. This furred angel was *her* messenger, he thought, the room must be that of Ruquel. And he longed to see her there, for an instant, for she was safe enough at that distance from him, he was not vital enough as yet to go after her. She had been very beautiful, very gentle.

He must not try to reason where her room lay inside the house. In any case, there was the giant, thank God, to protect her. And the Jew . . . surely the Jew was a magician.

As he patrolled the courtyard, Raoulin kept thinking of Ruquel, as of something precious he could never hope to see or touch, some prize once within his grasp, and now lost for ever, like the hope of Heaven. And added to this forfeiture there came to be the remembrance of his family, his friends, the university, the City, time, youth, and the world.

Then he sat down on the plot of grass beside the well, and he cried, and he was so weak his body was rocked and racked with it, this grief. But all the while, even as he wept these scalding tears, he sensed the other, waiting, *waiting there*, within him, for the hour he would belong to it and exist only to achieve its will.

'Sieur, you've been my saviour. I thank you for my life. But I don't see why you let me keep it. For I believe you know why I shouldn't be let live.'

These were the first conscious sentences he rendered the Jew.

They met in a parlour above the hall, about lamp-lighting, and the scent of flowers came in from the house vine, and olibanum from the antique lamp. There were a great many books, and some scrolls and ornate cases of leather. The two men sat facing each other over a table where there was wine to drink neither had touched.

'In honesty, Raoulin, I do know, for you spoke of it asleep, and I took the liberty to interrogate you.'

'And that – *it* – did it answer you also?'

'Not in words. It has no use for those. But it was aware, I think, in its primordial way, of our dialogue. Consider, it has no intelligence, only an instinct and an appetite. Even so, it may employ such knowledge as you yourself possess, to gain its ends. This is a power of desire more pliant and enduring than any of the desires of a man. It is a demon.'

'A demon. Yes.'

'I know its race, even. Out of Assyria, an *utuk*, having as its own form the body of a man, the head of a bird, but a bird of the beginnings, scaled not feathered, from the fifth day of the earth.'

Raoulin shuddered.

'Did I tell you all *her* story, too?'

'I have pieced it together. All your story and all the story of Helise d'Uscaret, who died and left her body for the demon to inhabit. For the matter of that, I sent Liva as a spy to the d'Uscaret mansion. He says the old kitchen woman and the groom go on about their doings as if nothing's amiss. I conjecture that what you left upon that bed crumbled entirely, even to the bones. If they think anything, there, perhaps it's that you and she have gone off together, in the way of heedless lovers.'

Raoulin said, 'That must come. Where else can I go but after her, into the grave and down to perdition.'

The Jew replied, 'God made all things. Even the creatures of his servant, the Devil. We are instructed to note the lesson their existence teaches. He never says we must offer them our throats.'

'Do you suppose I might prevent it – by abstaining? Heros made himself a priest, but the Devil won. My blood's hotter than the blood of Heros. And when it works in me like yeast – '

'There now,' said the Jew. And he poured out the crystal wine, and gave it to Raoulin, as if it were medicine. 'This is a clever enemy. It adapts itself as any beast will do. The ways of it are various. It can erupt inward, changing the victim to the semblance of itself, thereafter enacting by that body all it wishes. Or it passes into the body of a woman at intercourse, and her child, when it comes forth, will be the shell of the demon. It can do both, or either. It can lie down dormant too, even as with Helise, where it waited inside the womb, that terrible ambush ten years old. Only the key is constant, the procreative spasm. All the pure line of d'Uscaret were susceptible to it, but it can casually infect anywhere. Now that whole house has perished, only you are left to it. How can it let you die? It resisted the death of Helise until its transference was accomplished. The stabbing you gave yourself was sewn up in a day. I partly believe you might burn yourself alive, Raoulin, and this creature would find some means to build you up again. Death's no answer.' The Jew sipped his wine. 'Neither abstinence from the carnal act. The *utuk* provokes and seduces others to provoke. As you say, you're not proof against it.'

The dark was in the windows now. Hesperus rang from a nearby convent. The nights were lengthening and drawing near.

'How can there be any escape?'

Haninuh looked at him steadily.

'You will have decided, perhaps, I'm versed in certain arts.'

'A magician.'

'If you will call it so.'

'Then – can you cast this out of me?'

'Once before,' said Haninuh, 'it came, this thing, to mock me. I was unready then, knowing not enough. But after that failure, I studied in the school of demons, gathered together books, and artifacts from the Roman time here, when this began. Strange to say, I felt that the *utuk* would return to duel again with me. We're ancient foes. Its primal memory and mine contain rank seeds of all those battles. The cities of the desert, the chariots, and the chains. Yes, I suppose I can cast it out of you.'

Raoulin started up. The Jew stayed him.

'This isn't without great danger.'

'I'm ready to die,' said Raoulin. 'You know as much.'

'Also you must give yourself into my charge. What must be done is in itself unholy. There will be for you shame, rank sweetness, confusion, and agony. You may die indeed, you may lose your mind for ever. But this I do promise, *not* your soul.'

Raoulin stood before him, white-faced, arrogant with fear and courage. In the dusky lamplight, his eyes were only black.

'Sieur magus, do what you must. I'm your slave. When will it be?'

'In seven days, that is the new moon, God's remaking. Then.'

The Beautiful Jewess, eighteen years of age, sat playing with her cat on the floor of the bedroom. The cat's play was more sedate than it had been, still adept.

Haninuh, having been admitted, stood gazing at them.

He saw the child clearly, as the kitten was still visible in the cat. But both were mature, and changed. Ruquel was a woman. He must acknowledge that.

Presently she looked up, and her smile faded into a serene strictness. It was his own habitual look, given back to him like a mirror.

'I've read the book, as you instructed, my father.'

'That's good.'

'You've spoken to the young man?' He was touched at her way of referring to Raoulin, as if she were by far the elder. In some ways she was. Raoulin had not been wise, but he had, in the end, striven to be virtuous, prepared to sacrifice himself for the sins of other men.

'We've spoken. It shall be done.'

'And I?' she said. He was thankful for her quickness.

'As it's set down in the book.'

She lowered her eyes. Her face shadowed with the self-consciousness of the girl she was. Then the woman governed the girl, she looked up again and said, 'Yes, I'm willing. And I have the skills.'

'I know what's asked of you,' he said. 'Such a dance, though part of your secret training as in the days of Salomé, is a hidden thing. If you refused, I should have had to find some other, a paid dancer, and perhaps she doesn't exist in this City. Those that tutored you know of none.'

'Besides the paid one could command no magic.'

He had always allowed her that word, though it was not exactly accurate; it seemed to step appealingly from her tongue. She had from the first recognised she must be careful of its use with strangers.

'That's true, she could not. But let me say this, too. I'd never have petitioned you, my own daughter, except,' he hesitated, wanting to spare her, yet sure that there must be no lies, 'except, Ruquel, that I noticed at once you love this man, love him as your bridegroom, and your husband.'

She waited, and then she said, 'You'll think me foolish.

It happened the moment I saw him there. Perhaps even before, hearing the jar break on the street. He was at my door.'

'How should I think you foolish, Ruquel? You are a sybil. Your awareness has always been profound, even as a child. This love you have recognised, but not invented.'

'I honour you. I'd do nothing against my father's wishes.'

'I know. It is your father instead requests of you a dishonourable task, which only your love for Raoulin can redeem. You understand, despite everything, he may die?'

'Yes.'

'You understand, though I can protect you by the powers I command, in this arena nothing is certain? We are bound to it by our gifts and his plight. There's peril for all.'

'Yes.'

'You understand, my daughter, you are my star?'

'Yes,' she said, smiling again, 'I understand.'

Raoulin fasted on honey and curds and water, then on water only. The irritating hunger dissipated to a comfortable lack of all thought of food. Then he was cleansed with a potent cathartic herb. On the sixth day, the water was brought in a water-like goblet of glass. There was a drug mixed in it. His senses became abnormally clarified. His body was light, nearly weightless. He could smell the scent of flowering things and decaying things from streets away. He felt he could have reached up and clasped the vault of the sky.

That night, he supposed he would not be able to sleep at all, for everything had become so fascinating and had such nuances, even the creak of the mattress under him. But sleep discovered him and took him away up among the stars. He saw the City far below, he saw *stars* beneath him. When he woke at sunrise, he believed his soul had flown close to Heaven, and God had not flung him down.

Late in the seventh day, the woman brought him a bitter-sweet resinous drink. When he had consumed it, every doubt or fear he had had abandoned him. It was like strong wine, but without wine's blurring or analgesic properties, without wine's stupidity.

When Liva entered and asked that Raoulin go with him, Raoulin got up and did so, in a wild, still peace that was better than hope.

Nevertheless, Raoulin did not seem to take in the route they went by. Perhaps it only appeared irrelevant at that intrinsic moment.

Liva had brought him to a heavy double door of black wood, not ebony, something more essential, some tree that had altered into coal.

In the door were two handles of cold translucent onyx.

Liva had gone away. Raoulin gripped the door handles and turned them, one to the left and one to the right, or rather they seemed to turn themselves this way at the pressure of his hands.

Within, was midnight, without a star. But the Jew had already impressed upon him that he would come to the chamber and must go in. In he walked, and thrust the doors shut at his back.

Then there was nothing. Only the void.

There was only formlessness and darkness, but then the moon and the sun rose, and divided the day from the night.

After the great lights, came the fish and fowl like patterns, and the beasts and cattle, and there were mountains and valleys and enormous seas, and clouds and winds and stars, but in the end, men and women travelled across the plains, and he saw them though they had no names.

After this, he was aware he lay upon a mountain's top. A million miles high, gleamed the crescent moon, like the bow of a *kinnor*.

On all sides, granite, obsidian, salt, the mountain slid to a wilderness.

He knew the loneliness of a single being upon the huge

plate of the universe, who can only reach out to God.

His soul seemed to yearn upward. A vast silent finger brushed his forehead. Maybe it was only the wind in that place.

For hours he lay and marvelled, free of anything, and nearly free of self, lying there upon the stone of the mountain, with all night above.

Until, miles off, he heard the murmur of a drum.

He knew it, had heard it often. He tried to guess what it might be or mean. Then he realised that it came always nearer, that the beat intensified, and rumbled in the rock below him, and so strummed upward through his body and his bones.

He became aware of his body. Not any one portion of it, but every inch of flesh, each tier of the recumbent skeleton. The soles of his feet, his legs and thighs, the torso, neck and ears, the arms, the fingertips, the face, the scalp, even the hair, the teeth and nails, even the inner canals, links, crevices, membranes and nerves, each had a sentience, was possessed of a complete conscious concentrating awareness, yet it had life only through him.

The drum he identified now as a heartbeat. Every particle of his body, so autonomous yet so involved with *him*, responded to its rhythm.

The feeling was of a wonderful totality, and self-knowledge.

It was only then that he began to discern the chamber which contained the mountain top.

It was itself night-black. Its ceiling was enamelled with constellations, and figures of the zodiac, set out in all their stars, and through this the upper heaven glowed, and the new moon, resting upon Aquarius.

No walls upheld this ceiling.

The ground of the mountain was figured over on its blackness. Done in silver, like the sky, a five-pointed star seemed extending to infinity. And within it, a seven-pointed star had been fitted, and within that again, a star of three points, a triangle.

At the three points of the triangle, to each of which somehow he could see, was a smoking silver brazier formed as an animal. All were unnatural. To the north, at the apex, stood a winged bull with a lion's head, from this the smoke rose white; to the west was a silver calf with the sun on its forehead, it had the tongue of a snake, the smoulder from this was nacreous; east was a scorpion or scarab-thing, with the head of a man horned and bearded like a goat's, the steam from this one was transparent, remarkable only by a scintillant tremor in the air.

Within the triangle lay Raoulin, with his arms stretched up above his head towards the west and east points, his feet together pointing to the northern tip.

From the braziers came a mingling aroma, of balsam and hypericum, myrrh and orris.

In his ears he heard the rush of the perfumed smoke, and over and beneath, the drumbeat.

He felt no curiosity. He had no thoughts. He was utterly aware, cognizant, content.

A silver-white ewe came picking daintily over the rocks, some way beyond the stars which contained him, up on a peak in the sky. On her brow was a shining ray. She went around the wall of darkness, and was gone.

Then he heard two heartbeats, two drums. Another being, another life, was with him on the mountain.

Something uncurled, stretched itself within him. It was pleasant, had no urgency. He lay inside the triangle, his arms to the east and west, his feet pointing north, attentive.

There was a sudden sensation, like a kiss, on his breast above the heart. It did not startle him, he seemed almost to have expected it. After a moment, it came again, alighting over his ribcage, winging away. The touch was delightful and provocative, he longed for it to be repeated. For a while, nothing, and then, the kiss fell once more, more lingeringly, at his throat, and even as his skin tingled from it, again, over the nipple of his right side, so a string of fire was plucked there. After this, like a fine rain, the kissing came down glittering all across him. In a moment his whole body had become a lyre, sinuously strummed and vibrating – the rain of unseen sprites, to whom clothing was no barrier, fastened on him, their lips and fingers testing every atom of flesh and muscle, the framework of bone, for its potential pleasure. Even beneath him the rock itself seemed to give rise to these quivering entities.

Under the onslaught, he found he was unable to move, like one chained, at the mercy of the incorporeal delicious torture.

Dizzily his eyes remained fixed upon the rock in the sky, from which the second heartbeat seemed to have arisen. He could not apparently keep closed his eyes, though waves of sensation continually drove him to do so.

No, he could not close his eyes, and now upon the rock peak he saw a moon with a woman's face, which hung there and regarded him, shameless, helpless as he lay. And as the moon stared, the beings which fastened on him stripped him naked, as if for her cajolement, as if to bare him to her light.

But the moon . . . had black hair, and a head-dress of silver discs which she shook with a sound that matched the sinful rain that kissed him.

The moon had a black cloak. She had white hands that stole out as the hands stole upon him, that made little motions like the circling and flittering of those that played upon his body.

He could not look away from her. (And yet, just then, at a distance, the ends of the earth, he saw a male figure was standing, with his back turned to the moon in her cloak, his head averted both from this and from the naked man bound inside three stars. The figure perhaps had folded its arms across its chest, a wand in either hand, and before him was a kind of shallow basin upturned, or hollow mirror –)

But the moon had a cloak, and she cast it from her. She was all a woman, clad in a garment of silver scallops that covered her from the neck to the wrists and the ankles.

And then, on her arched bare feet, to the rhythm of the drumbeats, one faster, one slower and in counterpoint, she commenced a dance.

It was the dance of a snake. A swaying liquid coiling and uncoiling, like that of a river let along the ground. The arms followed the torso to and fro, the feet scarcely moved. It was not a spectacular or frenzied dance. It was immensely lambent, deeply suggestive and descriptive of the body of a woman, immeasurably cunning. It was the dance of Salomé before the king, which had hypnotised and driven him mad, and brought her, on a salver, the severed head of Jehanus. It was the dance of a snake.

As the languid pulses wove, the silver scallops began to drip away. Under them was a garment of thin stuff, perhaps byssus.

The shoulders of the dancer, her arms, rose from the silver like those of a maiden ascending from water.

Over the shoulders of the bound man, the unseen hands curved back and forth, to the pits of the arms, the line of the ribs, the flared points of the breast, and along the abdomen and the belly, like streams into the restless pounding groin.

As the silver rained off from the girl who was the snake, the rain poured on Raoulin, the torrent of hands and mouths. They stroked him, they teased and tickled him, they ran like threads of moltenness across his skin, over and beneath him. They had woken the root of life. He ached with lust and became lust, played, tautened, tuned, caressed by waters and airs and fire – and the drumbeat galloped, galloped, and the scales quickened like leaves and guttered from the girl's body wrapped in its second byssus skin. But the byssus too worked gradually away from her, unfurling like the calyx of a flower, slipping from her breasts that were the cups of flowers, that now hid themselves again, that now

were again and utterly unveiled, flowers starred with
flowers, while the kisses of invisible lips visited like moths
and tongues probed like trickles of silk, and hands feathered
and persuaded and the girl was naked to her loins dancing
upon the silver leaves of her dress, and the byssus unseamed
like snakeskin and slid away like water from the moon belly
with its tiny drop of shadow, the goblet of black hair, the
stemmed thighs smooth like alabaster –

In this instant Raoulin, who had forgotten his own name,
felt a terrible resistance, some clutch upon the choking pump
of desire, which strangled –

Unable to move, his lust thrashed, trying to burst from
the swollen blazing rod –

(And the figure he had not properly seen, and had also
forgotten, the figure which did not look at the dancer or the
naked man, this figure now stretched out the wands in his
hands and touched the metal surface before him. He spoke.
The words made no sound. Instead they shouted out in the
air above the triple stars of five and seven and three points.)

> *Evil One show thyself and come forth!*
> *O dweller among ruins and maker of ruins*
> *Get thee up to where thy ruins are;*
> *For the Lord God has sent me*
> *He has elected me his priest in this,*
> *He has given into my hands the Seven Powers*
> *According to the word of the sixth Day.*
> *Evil One, Foul One, show thyself and come forth!*

And the snake dancer rippled her hands along her silver
body and tore it in two pieces, flinging both aside, to reveal,
under the third veil, the nude skeleton.

The stifled death-throe of ecstasy was pierced by a
white and screeking pin. It came from inside the young
man's loins. It rent its way through him, through the
pelvis, spermary, and phallus. It was a birth. It thrust
in surges similar to the birth-pangs of a woman. It

seemed to rip his genitals like the beak of a vulture.

He cried, every prayer and blasphemy, every obscenity and childish plea he had ever known. Then he only screamed.

Strand by strand the rope of agony was pulled out of him.

It began as a jet of sheer semen, opalescent in the uncanny light. But the fountain rose and did not slacken or end. The moonstone gush travelled upward, spilling with a fearful elasticity, forming into a springing plume.

Until in its turn the plume, of a substance now composed not of any mortal sexual fluid, but of some astral plasmic material, coalesced, ran inward, began to construct another shape.

The chamber of night had gone all to blackness again. It was once more the void. But in the void, terror was made manifest.

Recreated without flesh, it was colourless, and dully shining. It had the limbs and torso of a man, yet lacking the procreative organ. It was winged. The head was the head of a bird of prey. As it was now, there were no eyes, only two sumps of cloudy darkness. It had no brain, this dark was not that.

Alone upon its stage it stirred, the bird head looked about with the un-eyes. It was seeking for what had been delivered of it, and for what had brought it forth.

Out of the black the figure of the magician Haninuh again grew visible. The two wands were gone from his hands, splintered at the impact of egression. But before him still there lay on the air the hollow length of metal. It was a shield of highly polished hide, iron-bound and gilded, with the lightnings and burning staff, from which stared a Medusa: a Roman relic of Par Dis.

In the left eye of the Medusa glimmered a bit of quartz, or flawed corunda. It, like the demon, had no longer any colour.

Haninuh straightened himself. He stood in the void and showed the shield before the demon.

'Come *thou*,' said Haninuh, 'for here thou art.'

Then the demon spat and sizzled and swirled towards the shield of Retullus Vusca, and into the Medusa's eye – which like itself had waited, waited: cut by the stroke of suicide from the entrails where, undissolved, this one piece had nestled like a child, washed out by blood under the hand of the dying Roman, thrust by him into the broken socket of the Medusa, his warning, all he could give, a jewel that was an eye – the *utuk* fell crackling, and met the shield, the eye, the gem, roared – like wind or fire – and was gone.

The Jew bent a little, leaning on the shield after his battle, to see where the jewel-fragment lay, erupted from its setting of eleven centuries. The shield seemed battered at last, brittle, like clinker. And for the jewel itself, it was like a cinder rendered up from the common hearth.

Haninuh spoke a Word over that cinder. Then he spoke a Word to the chamber and the blackness. To God he could not speak. For this, there were no words.

The embers of a morning lay in the green tines of the cedar tree. It seemed a dove was murmuring there.

'Oh that you were my brother that nursed at my mother's breast. When I should find you I might kiss you, it would be no shame. I would bring you into the house and there feed you on fruit and quench your thirst with wine. His left hand under my head, his right hand caressing me, he will teach me love.'

Raoulin's lids lifted. Beauty sat by the bed and looked at him with gentle sombre eyes. In colour, no blacker than his own.

'Who is this,' she said, 'coming out of the desert, leaning upon her love? Under the tree I woke you; let it be as the place where you were born.'

He was so weak he could not move, could not even speak to her. But he had never thought to see her again. He attempted, and failed, to find some means to offer her his voice.

She shook her head, and touched his lips with her fingers.

Upon the bed itself a striped cat stared at him, pitiless, guileless, angelic, and kneaded his feet.

He slept once more, comforted under their gaze.

Folded in a parchment, corded with seven charms, the amulet, or what remained of it, was buried in a clod of earth the size of a boy's hand. This then was packed into a box of horn, and that box into another of iron. Between the two boxes was a space, where an alchemical substance, being intruded, began of itself to burn. The iron box was closed, and put into a tablet of lead.

The whole was then carried to the midnight bank of the river, half a mile below Our Lady of Ashes, and thrown far out by the mighty arm of Liva. The tablet sank.

It sank, perhaps, to the mulch of the river's bottom, to wait once more, now for the deterioration of its containers, horn and iron and lead, earth, air, fire, and water. To wait out the river too, maybe, until that vast elder Leviathan of Paradys should shrink to a few puddles under some future sun. By then, the life of the amulet might also be eroded. If not, in that unpredictable to-come, some wandering one in the dry river-bottom would stoop and take up a lustreless stone, curious, and find the Devil still kept his court in the world. But possibly that day would never be.

For Raoulin, he was a very long time ill in the house of Haninuh. But being excellently, and cleverly and lovingly, tended, recovered before winter sealed the City in its orb of ice.

In the spring letters went from Raoulin to his kindred at the northern farm. But then the happiness turned like cream. For Raoulin had set himself to become a Jew by faith, conceivably more orthodox than his mentor. The reasons that he gave were unhelpful, for the actual spur had risen in him as fiercely and insatiably as young blood.

(Perhaps too he remembered a Christian priest under the Sacrifice, who had turned from him in his hour of horrible need.)

But his family cast off Raoulin. That was that.

Among the scholars of Haninuh's fraternity, this scholar found more than enough to study, and took to these new tutors, these new arcane formulae, with greed. For themselves, the Jews were kind to him. Even in Paradys, in their hearts, they reckoned their way was the only one, and had grown used to the insults and cruelties this knack provoked. For the gentile who approached them from the night, innocent, quietly asking, they could not but feel some wondering affection. As he grew in stature among them, they came to speak of their foundling with pride.

By then, of course, he had wed Ruquel, Haninuh's exquisite daughter, under the canopy.

These two knew together more happiness than most, less pain than many. They seldom spoke of death. Like the draining of the river, such things were the concern of God.